FIGHTBACK

Fightback

Published by The Conrad Press Ltd. in the United Kingdom 2022

Tel: +44(0)1227 472 874
www.theconradpress.com
info@theconradpress.com

ISBN 978-1-914913-80-8

Printed and bound in Great Britain by Clays Ltd, Elcograf S.p.A

Typesetting and cover design by The Book Typesetters
www.thebooktypesetters.com

The Conrad Press logo was designed by Maria Priestley.

1.

East London Gazette (2018)

Certain areas in East London are now beset by criminal gangs engaged in knife crime, drugs, and other criminal acts. Due to stringent government cuts, the police appear to be fighting a losing battle...

He was freezing cold, his feet as cold as blocks of ice with drips hanging off the end of his nose. Albert Oxford trudged his weary way back from the stadium. His team had played poorly conceding a soft goal to a team they should have beaten comfortably.

The chill wind cut through him and only the scarf, woollen flat-cap, gloves and extra layers of clothing were helping to save him from hypothermia. The prospect of a Saturday night in an empty house did not fill him full of the joys of spring, or in this case, the joys of mid-winter.

After Lizzie's death a year ago from a rotten, horrible disease, the days and, especially the evenings, were difficult. She had been suffering for over a year and her death came as a relief to him, and her, as he hated seeing her suffering and wasting away morphing from a fit and healthy, fun loving, caring woman to a skeletal wretch who had to have constant care almost twenty-four hours a day. She had been inclined to see the good in everything whereas Albert tended to be more cynical and treated people outside his circle, generally, with a great deal of suspicion.

As he neared home, he had a choice of using the park as a shortcut to save him walking an extra four hundred yards or sticking to the lit streets. The problem with the park was that at this time of night the lighting was at a minimum because of Council cuts and savings and Albert knew what feral types frequented the park. He wasn't thinking about just the foxes and stray cats.

Striding on purposely he turned into the park. Although the lighting was practically non-existent, he was still able to make out shapes near the clump of trees on his left. Three large oak trees and a scattering of horse chestnut trees gave that area of the park a foreboding, menacing look.

Two bicycles lay on their sides while a group of five or six hooded youths appeared to be in deep conversation. This was occasionally punctuated by raucous bouts of laughter. He was anxious not to be spotted. Albert picked up his pace and was relieved when he placed his key in his street door and entered his abode.

How things had changed since Lizzie had passed away. Instead of an aroma of a chilli con carne or a spaghetti bolognese, the house remained in darkness until Albert switched on his hallway lighting. And instead of a polite enquiry from Lizzie as to how his team had played there was now a silence.

The terraced three-bedroom ex-council house was now theirs, or his, to be factually correct. Lizzie's late father had left them a small legacy, which, coupled with their own industry, and Lizzie's astute economics, enabled them to call this particular part of east London their own.

Once he had sat down with a large glass of red, Albert sank into deeper self-pity mode fairly quickly. Alone and living in a desperate part of London and with no ambition, or inclination to move, he examined his prospects. He was now in his early fifties and was a part-time black cab driver, earning enough money to get by. By renting a cab from Ray, who lived a couple of streets away, he was able to earn as much as he needed.

The east end of London was somewhat different to what it was 40 years ago, with gangs of uncontrollable youths terrorising ordinary people attempting to get on with their lives. Uncontrolled immigration had brought certain parts of London to its knees and the underfunded and under-staffed police were struggling to cope. Some decent people were too frightened to go outside the confines of their houses. What a state of affairs!

Another glass of Malbec was followed by another and after blearily trying to watch where his team went wrong on Match of the Day, Albert wearily hauled himself upstairs to bed. Sleep, however, was a stranger, as the night was punctuated by fireworks, screams and police sirens. In other words, a fairly normal Saturday night.

2.

Sunday did not dawn bright and Albert could hear cars and buses sloshing through puddles of water but, nevertheless, he promised himself that he would perform his weekly Sunday ritual by walking Mo's dog, Buddy. Mo was his elderly neighbour who lived opposite. Mo Connors had been widowed ten years ago and Albert never saw a lot of her, apart from an occasional peek from behind her net curtains. She very rarely ventured outdoors and was not the greatest conversationalist in the world. She was an elderly woman in her early eighties, diminutive in stature and nearly always wore the same dull cardigan and dark skirt. By the time Albert knocked on Mrs. Connor's door the rain had relented.

Good morning, Mrs. Connors,' said Albert from the doorstep. No reply, just a proffered hand which held a dog-lead, to which was attached a mixture of dog breeds, all bound into one body, but which had a fiercely wagging tail. The dog had realised who was at the door.

'Come on boy, let's see what delights are waiting for us in Dogshit Park.' So named by Albert, due to the number of pet owners who refused to pick up their dog's mess.

On the way to the park Albert had to walk down a short street with no houses fronting onto the street. It contained just a couple of lock-up garages. Because there were no CCTV cameras on this street an inordinate amount of rubbish was abandoned by lazy sods who couldn't be bothered to take it to the local council recycling tip.

Picking his way through the garbage, Albert saw Lech cleaning his work van. Lech was an immigrant Pole who now had his own cleaning business and was one of Albert's drinking companions in the Princess Victoria. A giant of a man with a thick torso and large square face with unkempt, brown tousled hair which was turning grey at the sides. Albert used the Princess Victoria on a Sunday lunchtime and had been doing so for some years and he found the big Pole, Lech, an ideal drinking companion, especially as he bought his round when required. The two men shared the same views regarding the yob culture which had developed in their part of town. They also agreed that the area had gone downhill rapidly in the last few years.

'Will I see you later, Lech?' Albert asked the huge Pole.

'For sure, your team useless,' replied Lech in fractured English.

'I will buy you a pint if you don't talk about football.'

'That is a good deal for me, Albert,' replied Lech.

Progressing onwards, Albert and Buddy entered the park. The park was the same one that Albert had walked through some fourteen hours ago but had taken on a different appearance. No dark gloomy shapes or shadows on this occasion Albert allowed the dog a bit of freedom from the leash knowing that he would come back when called. The secret was that Albert's left-hand pocket contained some dog treats and Buddy knew that by returning he would be rewarded. Buddy did his business. It was scooped up by Albert and was disposed of.

Albert was, as usual, dismayed by what he saw. Used syringes, the odd used contraceptive, a pile of discarded laughing gas cylinders and of course, the obligatory supermarket trolley on its side. Until the park keepers attended on the following Monday, the park would contain a detritus of waste and flotsam. Nevertheless, the dog enjoyed his walk. He sniffed and constantly wagged his tail. After all, Buddy wouldn't be worried about the state of the park, this was his Garden of Eden.

Albert returned a grateful Buddy to his not-so-grateful owner. Albert returned home to shower and change before his Sunday ritual at the Princess Victoria public house.

Sunday lunchtimes in the Princess Victoria were lively and very busy. An excited chatter could be heard above the jukebox and clatter of glasses. The public house was deceptively cosy with a fake log fire churning out a generous heat. The assorted oak tables and red padded fake-leather chairs were mainly occupied near the fireplace. The wooden oak topped bar was spotless, with the brass fittings and pumps polished to within an inch of their lives. The bar sported half a dozen different pumps, all of them poised to dispense foaming draughts of ale.

The publican was a larger-than-life character called Eddie. He was a man of average height but with a huge paunch that would befit a publican who enjoyed sampling his own wares. He sported massive forearms and had huge hams for hands with fingers as thick as prime sausages. He always wore a pair of glasses which had been repaired numerous times and had the habit of being misplaced. This caused much mirth in the pub when Eddie went on a 'glasses-finding' expedition. At that moment they were perched on the end of his nose. A publican all his life after being invalided out of the army, Eddie would enthral any listeners about his experiences in the war although most knew that the nearest Eddie got to a battlefield was from inside the catering tent at the training complex at Aldershot.

So Private Eddie Baines was a cook and dishwasher. However, Eddie's stories were great fun. Customers revelled in tales of Eddie's made-up adventures in the Middle East and Northern Ireland. If Eddie Baines was to be believed, he alone, was responsible for huge damages suffered by the Taliban and the Irish Republican Army, respectively. In truth, Private Eddie Baines probably inflicted more damage on his own troops with his cooking skills. He was, though, a magnanimous host. Apart from buying his favoured customers the odd pint, Eddie maintained an East End tradition of laying on snacks such as roast potatoes, or cheese and biscuits. Always rapidly devoured, these treats were replaced almost as quickly as they were cleared by the locusts who made up the pub clientele. Eddie was also part of the group that had become dismayed by the area's decline into abject mediocrity.

'Your team were shit yesterday, Albert,' said Eddie. At that point the big figure of Lech appeared behind Albert

12

and he said to Eddie,

'Eddie. No mention of football and Albert will buy you beer.' Albert then bought beer for Eddie and Lech.

Joining them at the end of the bar was a tall, thin man in his forties. Smartly dressed in a jacket, collar and tie, Albert only knew him as Mark. He did not live locally but arrived at the pub later than Albert and his companions. He always left after drinking a couple of pints and departed well before the others. He seemed to enjoy Albert and Lech's company and was always asking about the area.

'Did you go to the game yesterday?' Mark asked Albert. Albert bought Mark a pint.

Long before Albert left the pub to return home, Mark had already disappeared after buying his round.

'He's a bit of a strange one, he's not from around here,' said Eddie.

'Yeh, there's something of the night about him,' Albert replied.

After his fill of roast potatoes, cheese and biscuits and three pints of foaming ale Albert returned to his three-bed-room, ex-council, terraced house to fall asleep in his comfortable armchair.

3.

Monday morning dawned and was the beginning of the week that was to have an effect on the rest of Albert Oxford's life.

As Albert walked the few streets to pick up the London Taxi that would be his workplace and office for the coming week, he contemplated his situation. Now a widower, he had no prospects of meeting anyone to settle down with. If the truth be known, he didn't want any other relationship, other than the one he had had with Lizzie. His only company centred around the pub and its customers. He lived in a depressed part of London plagued by yobs and gangs who were running wild. The taxi gave him the opportunity to earn enough to pay for his food and beer. Was that it? he asked himself. His two kids had both left home. His son was working in Dubai and his daughter was teaching in the north of England. Both of them were happily married. He hadn't seen either since the funeral and phone calls were almost non-existent except on his birthday, Father's Day and Christmas.

He spent a few hours shuffling the cab round London's blocked streets, swearing at the odd cyclist and engaging with punters in the back of the cab. This activity earned him his target money for the day. The journey home was fractious due to rush-hour traffic and an accident blocking traffic coming out of the City.

Before handing the taxi back to Ray for his night shift, Albert always made sure that he had replaced the diesel he had used. He pulled into a petrol station a few streets away from Ray's address.

Albert filled up with diesel, and he went inside the kiosk to pay. As he was leaving by the door which led onto the forecourt, he was pushed aside by a tall, well-built figure wearing a black hoodie with a white stripe running the length of each sleeve. The face was obscured by the hood.

Albert muttered something non-complementary under his breath and as he got back into the cab and started the engine, the hooded figure burst back out of the service station shop clutching a fistful of notes which he stuffed into the pocket of his denim jeans.

Hood then ran to a Kawasaki motorbike on which sat a track-suited figure wearing a crash helmet. The motor bike engine was ticking over and when the Hood scooped up the crash helmet on the pillion passenger seat, the rider and the Hood started to move off on the bike with a loud revving of the engine.

Without thinking about any consequences, Albert engaged the drive gear of the automatic cab and shot forward to block the exit of the forecourt from the motor bike. The bike, in an effort to avoid Alberts taxi, slewed round the front end of the cab. This caused the rider to temporarily lose control. This resulted in his pillion passenger being dumped onto the hard concrete of the forecourt.

The hooded figure picked himself up and stared at Albert. During his fall, his crash helmet had been dislodged from his head. Albert found himself transfixed by a huge black head. the size of a football, with a yellow-metal ring piercing his nose. He must have been six foot, five inches tall and when he ran to be reunited with the bike and its rider, he ran with a pronounced limp. The motorbike roared off.

Albert safely parked the cab and ran into the service station. He stepped over some scattered coins. Albert saw an elderly Asian man lying on the floor outside his kiosk. He was bleeding from a cut above his left eye. Albert could see that he was conscious and asked him if he wanted an ambulance. The old man declined the offer but allowed Albert to call the police. Albert reassured him that they were on route. He left his mobile number with the attendant and left the kiosk to drive the cab back to Ray's.

Albert informed Ray what had just happened.

'No surprise, Albert, they park up near here when I finish my nightshift. I often think they're going to rob me but when I see them here, I get out of the cab pretending I'm adjusting a shoulder holster and make out I'm shooting at them by pointing my finger at them. The bottle-less bastards always fuck off.' Albert laughed and walked home.

On route he couldn't help thinking about the robbery he had just witnessed. What was scary was the fact that the robber had stared at him for what seemed an inordinate amount of time. Why would that be? Was it because Albert had had the insolence to attempt to block his exit path?

Once he was back inside the comfort of home, Albert microwaved his evening meal, a supermarket curry. A glass of red and then a change of attire followed as Monday evenings were spent with next-door neighbour, Harry.

Harry Prentice belonged to a working-men's club on the other side of Dogshit Park. He was a huge lump of a man and had recently retired from work as a porter and dogsbody at Smithfield Meat Market in the City of London.

Harry, as they say, had been around the block a few times and had been detained on a couple of occasions at Her Majesty's Pleasure for the odd bit of thieving and assault. Harry was no angel but had been a good neighbour to Albert and his late wife, Lizzie. He sported a vivid weal of a scar on his left cheek. His eyes always seemed to have a steely grey stare and he was the type you would not want to meet in a dark alley late at night.

The working men's club was a Monday night habit, watching whatever game of football was on the Sky Sports channel. On their way to the club Albert told Harry about the robbery he had witnessed. He described the hooded robber. Harry said, 'He's a local and he's one of the scum that hang around in the park near us. His limp is permanent cos apparently he got attacked by a dog once.'

Harry's knowledge of the area and the local lowlife stemmed from the fact that Harry wanted to keep up to date with what was going on in the immediate vicinity of his home. One of his convictions had been for assaulting a youth who had insulted his wife whilst returning from a night out in the West End of London. The victim had finished up in hospital with a couple of broken limbs and the victim had long left the hospital before Harry Prentice had completed a six-month prison sentence.

Albert had made sure that Harry's wife didn't want for anything while he was inside. He had even run her to the prison to visit Harry. This meant Albert forgoing a day's work in the taxi. It was a gesture Harry would always be grateful for.

The locals also tended to confide in Harry, knowing his past. With no hair, and a scar running from below his left eye to his chin, he was an instantly recognisable figure in the area. He was also a very popular man as he could be compassionate with those who respected him.

The facial scar had been the result of an attack by a group of youths. The attack had been unprovoked. If Harry Prentice knew who had done it, he wouldn't say but had always avowed that revenge would always be on the agenda and he was quite prepared to wait for his opportunity.

In the club they both watched the game, which was notable for its turgidity. Albert's mobile call from the police was almost a relief. The caller was attached to the CID at the local police station. Albert told the detective what he had witnessed and when asked whether he would recognise the robber again he replied that he didn't think that he could. The detective made an appointment with Albert for the following evening.

After the game finished, both men made their way back towards home, taking in the scenic route through Dogshit Park. As usual, a group of hoodies were just noticeable in the gloom.

'Look at them shitbags. A decent flamethrower is all

that's required,' said Harry.

4.

On Tuesday evening Albert was ensconced indoors when a young smartly dressed man wearing a dark-blue overcoat rang Albert's doorbell.

As soon as he had made his visitor comfortable in his living room, Albert repeated his story, save on this occasion Albert had a change of heart, and told young DC McEvoy that he thought he would recognise the robber again and provided McEvoy with a detailed description, including the nose ring. He thanked Albert for his help. Detective McEvoy told Albert he would be in touch.

An early night for Albert was disturbed by 2am fireworks, emergency service sirens and a host of dog barking which had been set off by the fireworks.

The following day was business as usual and unusually, a good day in the cab. Some of the customers even appeared human, and a few of them even provided a modicum of interesting conversation.

His last job was taking two Americans to Heathrow which meant Albert was going to be late dropping the cab off to Ray. Ray never ever minded a late drop off provided he got the call from Albert and so it was that the taxi, replenished with diesel, was dropped off outside Ray's house. After an exchange of pleasantries Albert set off for home. He decided to take the shortcut through Dogshit Park, probably against his better judgement, but he was already late for his glass of wine and microwaved meal.

Carefully avoiding a discarded stained mattress at the park entrance Albert's attention was drawn, even in the darkness, to a group of people standing near the wall to rear gardens away to his left. They were hovering by the dark shapes of the trees.

Head down, Albert ploughed on towards home when a loud voice roared in his direction, shouting,

'Stop! You! Oi, stop.'

Albert did not acknowledge the shouts and stepped purposely forward but was aware that at least two people were running after him. Albert quickened his pace and looked round to see the two shapes gaining on him. As they were nearly upon him, he tripped on the path edge and fell heavily onto the wet grass.

Immediately, Albert received a kick to his solar plexus followed instantaneously by a kick to his head. A flurry of kicks followed and Albert attempted to roll into a foetal position in an attempt to protect himself as much as possible. He cast a glance at his two attackers and to his dismay saw that the prime assailant was none other than the petrol station robber from the previous day, his metal nose ring glinting in the watery moonlight. There was a white stripe down each sleeve of his hoodie. The other attacker was a thin, sallow faced youth, of Asian origin, with a long thin nose. He was wearing a dark puffer jacket and, mercifully for Albert, black trainers which would lessen the damage on his body from the kicks.

On reflection afterwards Albert thought it was a huge mistake to look at his attackers as the frenzied onslaught continued with blows and kicks raining down on his body. Before losing consciousness, Albert could hear fireworks and dogs barking.

5.

When he awoke, Albert found he was lying in a bed which he thought was a room in the side wing of a hospital. Everything appeared to have been painted grey, which just happened to match the pallor of Albert's skin. Attached to the back of his wrist was a cannula and tubing. This supplied him with fluid and painkillers, presumably to soften the overriding feeling in his body, which was acute pain. It was hard to tell which hurt most, his stomach, head or back. A nurse hovered by his bed and Albert said, 'Where am I and how long have I been here?'

The nurse replied, 'Two days and you're in Whipps Cross Hospital.'

'When can I go home?' to which the nurse replied,

'When the doctor says you're fit to be released.' The nurse, being brick-built, wasn't going to be argued with, and said to Albert,

'I'm going to get you a light meal, but in the meantime you have two visitors. Do you want to see them?'

Albert replied, 'If it's the two that did this, then, no, I'll pass on that. Anybody else, I don't mind.'

Before the nurse left Albert asked her, 'Nurse, when I get

over this, will I be able to play the piano?'

'I've heard that one about a hundred times Mr. Oxford, but I'm pleased to hear that you haven't had a sense of humour by-pass.'

Albert's visitor was his Polish friend, Lech, accompanied by his wife Annelka.

Lech was visibly upset at his friend Albert's appearance.

'You look pretty bad, Albert. What happened?'

Albert told him everything including the descriptions of his two attackers. Lech said,

'I know these two scumbags. I see them walk past my van when they come out of the park. The big one, they call Trax, and the Asian is called Saf. They run a gang. They are like rats. They are not nice people. We need to hurt them badly, Albert.'

Albert said to him,

'Lech, I can't think of anything like that at the moment. All I want to do is get out of this place and get home.'

'I will speak to you, Albert, when you get home,' said Lech.

The following day Albert was seen by the duty doctor who told him that because of losing consciousness he would be kept in for another 24 hours in order that a head injury assessment could be undertaken. When Albert asked about his injuries the young fresh-faced doctor told Albert that he had two badly bruised ribs which would be quite painful for a couple of weeks. He had various bruises to his upper and lower body in line with being kicked and punched. The young doctor told Albert that if scans taken later that day proved satisfactory then he would be allowed to leave the hospital the next day. He added, 'And you can get back to playing your piano, Mr. Oxford.'

East London Gazette

A local man, Mr. Albert Oxford was attacked and assaulted in Dewdrop Park on Wednesday evening and was taken to Whipps Cross Hospital suffering from severe bruising. Police are appealing for any witnesses...

The following day Albert was picked up at the hospital by Lech's wife Annelka. After getting indoors Albert realised he was still in considerable pain. He thought the best place for him would be the safe haven of his bed but before climbing the stairs, the front doorbell rang. There stood DC McEvoy. The young detective was invited in.

'I'm investigating the attack on you in the park on Tuesday. Is there anything you want to tell me that would assist me in apprehending the offenders?'

Albert repeated what he had told Lech, saying, 'I'm sure it was the two who did the petrol station robbery. This must be their way of putting the frighteners on me. How did I end up in hospital?' Albert asked McEvoy.

McEvoy said, 'A local resident who lives on the far side of the park was putting out his dustbins when he heard the shouting and then saw you being attacked. He shouted out and released his German Shepherd dog who raced across the park towards your assailants. The taller one of the two got very agitated at the sight of the dog and both of your attackers ran off. The Good Samaritan then rang for an ambulance and naturally the police were informed. I was given the case by my Detective Inspector Marker as I had dealt with you as a witness for the petrol station robbery.'

Albert said, 'My attacker was the robber.'

McEvoy replied 'You saw a robber wearing a hood and your assault was in poor lighting. That evidence wouldn't stand up in court but what I promise you is that I will do some digging into this robber and his associate and keep you updated. At some stage I will need you to make a statement.'

Arrangements were made for Albert to make a statement to the police the following day at Forest Gate police station.

After a disturbed night's sleep Albert travelled by bus to Forest Gate Police Station where he supplied a statement to a young detective who looked even younger than McEvoy. He did not mention the names Trax or Saf but provided a description that covered the basics and nothing more. Albert was not confident in any shape or form that his two attackers would be prosecuted. He reflected back to what Lech had said at the hospital.

They need to be hurt, Albert. Lech was serious and Albert recalled how upset Lech appeared to be at the extent of his injuries. Albert was also aware that Lech's domestic cleaning business, which he operated out of his Ford transit van, had also been affected by gang members targeting his van.

Lech had found his windscreen smashed and on another occasion had discovered that all four of the tyres on the van had been slashed.

The more Albert thought about Trax and his mate, the more wound up he got, especially after McEvoy had intimated that there was not much chance of a prosecution.

6.

By the time Sunday had arrived, the pain of Albert's injuries had started to subside and he felt well enough to knock on Mo Connor's door. Mrs. Connor, not being much of a conversationalist, looked visibly shocked at the state of Albert's contusions. Buddy appeared behind her wagging his tail. Albert decided it was safe to confront the park as it was a Sunday morning and was bathed in bright winter sunshine. The dog as usual enjoyed his exercise and the fresh air.

Walking up the far side of the park Albert had a look at the houses bordering the park and tried to remember which of the houses was home to the German Shepherd. His first attempt was successful and a small bespectacled man in his seventies answered the doorbell. A loud bark could be heard from within. Albert said to the man,

'I just wanted to thank you for what you did the other night.' Looking very shocked at Albert's bruised face he replied,

'I couldn't believe what was happening. Normally I wouldn't get involved but I thought they were going to kill you. That's why I let Brian loose.'

'Brian?' Albert queried.

The old man said 'Don't ask. My wife's idea. It was me who called the ambulance.'

'What did you see of my attackers?' asked Albert.

'Look, with the best will in the world I don't want to get involved. Those types, yobs, whatever you want to call them, have been terrorising this neighbourhood for the last five years or so. People down this street have had their windows put in, vehicles vandalised, and they keep getting away with it.'

Albert asked him if they had reported any of these attacks to the police.

'What's the point?' asked the old man. 'Nothing would get done. Can you imagine what would happen to us if we had to give evidence in court?'

Albert thanked the man for calling the ambulance and returned Buddy to Mrs. Connors.

Albert's next port of call after returning the dog was to walk round to the Princess Victoria for his Sunday lunchtime pint. The first-person Albert saw was Eddie who looked visibly upset at Albert's appearance.

'Bloody hell, what a state you're in. They need sorting out, good and proper. Let me get you a pint.' A few regulars sidled up to Albert and expressed their sympathy. Their offers of a drink could have kept Albert in drink for some considerable time. Whilst having a sup of his pint of IPA, Lech wandered up behind Albert.

'How are the injuries, Albert?' he asked.

'Still pretty painful,' he replied.

Just after Lech, Eddie and Albert had discussed the previous day's football results the tall lean figure of Mark walked into the pub dressed immaculately as usual. He had an air of aloofness, a pinched face, protruding chin and angular nose. He sported a pair of spectacles worn on the end of his nose. Ordering himself a pint and making the offer of a drink to the others he asked Albert what had happened.

'Do they know who did it?' he asked Albert.

'I think they have a good idea, but I don't expect anything to happen. There is a mob running wild round here and nobody gives a damn.'

Mark didn't reply but got stuck into his pint.

Eddie's free food disappeared as quickly as it arrived and shortly afterwards Mark took his leave. After another pint, Albert walked home to his usual Sunday afternoon of sleep in the comfortable armchair.

His Sunday slumber was disturbed by his doorbell ringing. When he opened the door, there stood the figure of Mrs. Connors, looking very upset.

'Mr. Oxford, I need your help, Buddy has gone missing. He must have slipped out the front door when I put something in the dustbin. I didn't notice he was missing for about half an hour.'

Albert grabbed his coat and a torch and told Mo to wait indoors just in case Buddy returned home. Albert thought the first place to look would be the park where Buddy appeared to enjoy himself more. Although dark and fearful of the yobs frequenting the park, he still decided that the park would be his first port of call.

The early evening sky was starlit, with a full moon lighting the park up more than normal for that time of year. There was no sign of any human activity as Albert walked past two large horse chestnut trees.

Albert suddenly stopped dead in his tracks. Hanging from a large branch and swaying in the slight breeze was the obviously lifeless form of his regular walking companion, Buddy. The poor dog was suspended by a length of string which had been tied around his neck.

Distraught, Albert ran to Lech's front door and told him he needed his help and described what had happened. Lech grabbed a kitchen knife and he and Albert retraced the steps back to the tree where the swaying body of the dog stood out eerily in the moonlit expanse of the park.

Using the knife, Lech released the dog into Albert's arms. The dog was still warm, but obviously dead. Albert found himself crying into the dog's furry, beautiful head. The poor dog's eyes were open with a pleading look staring at Albert. Lech placed his arm around Albert and they walked back to Lech's address.

'I can't take the dog back to Mo and tell her this, Lech,' said Albert, 'I'm going to tell her he was knocked over by a car. What should we do with the dog?'

Lech replied, 'Albert, don't worry, I will take care of the dog. I will ring the vets or PDSA and make sure the dog is taken care of.'

'Somebody is fucking going to pay for this,' said Albert. The big Pole nodded in agreement.

They walked round the corner to Lech's van. He unlocked the sliding side door and carefully placed the dog on the floor of the van and covered him with a towel.

Although Albert was still very upset he still had another upsetting experience in front of him and that was to tell his elderly neighbour, Mo Connors, about the loss of her companion and friend. This he did, explaining that the dog had been hit by a vehicle and that Lech had taken care of the dog and that the dog had been catered for in a respectful manner. Old Mrs. Connors took the news badly, as expected, but still took time to thank Albert for his help. That was the most emotional that Albert had seen Mrs. Connors.

7.

The following week, Albert's injuries and pain had improved but what did not improve was Albert's state of mind. He was convinced that the death of the dog was caused by Trax and his gang but proving it would be impossible.

During the week, he called round to see Lech and was invited in. He was handed a fairly large measure of Krupnik, a sweet Polish liqueur based on vodka, which nearly knocked Albert off his feet. Lech smiled but then with a straight face, said to Albert,

'What are we going to do about our friends in the park? Everyone around here is shit scared of them,'

'The bad news is that the police can't, or won't do anything about them, so perhaps we will have to take care of them ourselves,' Albert replied.

The Krupnik flowed freely and adventurous plans were put forward and discussed until, at some stage, Albert was on the point of passing out in an alcoholic stupor. Lech walked Albert to his front door. Albert collapsed into bed dreaming of dogs hanging from trees, coupled with a big round black human head with a ring through a huge bulbous nose. The head was sneering at him.

Albert struggled awake with a beast of a hangover. Because of that, and because his bruised ribs still restricted full movement, Albert decided that today wasn't the day for sitting stewing in London's traffic. He spent a quiet morning indoors and decided that a livener was what was required, which meant a knock-on next-door neighbour Harry's door.

'Do you fancy a pint at the working men's club?'

Harry didn't need a second invitation and before long they were both ensconced in the warm confines of the club with a pint and a cheese and pickle sandwich. The club was frequented by regulars who lived locally and who lived on the street which faced onto the park. Harry was obviously a popular character in the club with numerous offers of drinks, all of which were declined with thanks. The buxom middle-aged barmaid approached Harry's table.

'Did you hear about that poor dog, Harry?' she asked in a whisper.

'No,' said Harry. 'What happened, Bella?'

Well, there's people saying that this gang, that's causing all the aggro around here, hung a dog from a tree.'

Harry shook his head and said, 'That's unbelievable, what sort of pigs would do that?'

Bella returned to the bar area and Albert said to Harry, 'I know about this, Harry. The dog belonged to Mrs. Connors who lives opposite us.'

'What? The dog you take for a walk on the weekend?'

Albert nodded and said,

'Yes, I didn't want to tell her what really happened as I didn't want to upset her. Lech, the Polish cleaning guy, helped me and got rid of the dog at the PDSA.'

'Who did it, Albert?'

'Bella was right. It's that feral mob who are terrorising everyone round here. One of them in particular, a huge black lump called Trax is turning into a monster. The Old Bill are not doing too much, making all sorts of excuses,' Albert replied.

'Is that the one with a ring through his nose, a big pile of shit?' asked Harry.

'That's him,' said Albert.

'When Libby was coming back from the shops the other day, he caught her looking at him. Just a glance, but he did no more than gob a load of phlegm at her feet and told her not to look at him. She was quite upset, obviously.'

'What a bastard!' Albert got quite upset at what had happened to Harry's wife, Libby. He finished his pint and told Harry that he was going to walk home. With a fair measure of bravado he decided to walk through the park. There was nobody in the park apart from one solitary dog walker. When Albert turned into his street, he saw Mo Connors at his front door. She looked very upset.

'Why didn't you tell me what happened to Buddy?'

Albert said, 'I didn't want to upset you anymore than was necessary. How did you find out what happened?'

'A woman I know from the supermarket told me about it. She said Buddy was hanging from a tree.' A tear slid down the cheek of Mo Connors. 'That dog would never have hurt a soul. You know that. He was a lovely dog.'

With that, Mrs. Connors turned and shuffled back into her empty house.

The next morning Albert walked to the town centre in Stratford to pay money into his local bank. The money consisted of a couple of weeks' taxi earnings and that would enable his bank to meet his standing orders for household amenities. Albert made sure he had enough left to pay for his beer and food. Albert had a few pounds stashed away in a floor safe. Money that he had managed to avoid paying to Her Majesty's Customs and Excise, after careful discussion with his taxi accountant. Money for a rainy day, as some would say.

He made his way back through the shopping centre. He despaired at the sight of rough sleepers in abandoned shop doorways, covered by newspapers, cardboard and smelly, dirty blankets. His exit path was punctuated by an assortment of dishevelled human menagerie, begging from fellow passers-by. They proffered a dirty polystyrene cup asking for money. Some had the obligatory dog tied to themselves with a bit of string and had a crudely written piece of cardboard highlighting their plight. Albert could not help thinking about all those radio talk show hosts and precious television presenters who pontificated from their ivory towers that the problems in the inner city were not as bad as people described.

Let them come down here and live for a couple weeks, thought Albert.

As Albert made his way home along the back-doubles, a dark car pulled up alongside him. The driver leant across and opened the passenger door and said to Albert,

'Jump in.'

Recognising DC McEvoy, Albert slid into the passenger seat.

'Mr. Oxford, this meeting is unofficial. I'm speaking to you from a completely neutral position. We are aware of what is happening in your area and I agree that the situation is getting out of control, but we have neither the resources, nor any witnesses willing to give evidence or to stand up to the troublemakers. We know about the dog but people in your area are running scared of this mob. The reason I'm telling you this is because you must be wondering why we haven't done anything about this but as I've said, with no witnesses or people willing to help us, our hands are tied.'

'Who are they? And how did you know about the dog?' asked Albert. McEvoy pulled off the street into a shop forefront and switched off the engine. He took out a sheet of paper and said,

'I can't let you have this but the gang from the park are not just terrorising your area. We are looking to build up a team to tackle them, but it is taking time and, quite frankly, we are struggling with resources such as personnel, money and overtime budgets. My governors are getting it in the neck from the hierarchy at Scotland Yard and are threatening us that something has to be done. We've been told that if the situation does not improve there will be no promotions and some of us will have to think about our futures as far as having a job is concerned. My Detective Inspector, Dave Marker is extremely concerned about the local situation and is taking an active interest in everything that is going on. As for knowing about the dog, I have a few contacts in the local community, people who will tell us snippets but don't want to get involved because of the possible consequences.'

'Why are you telling me this?' asked Albert.

'I shouldn't be telling you any of this, but my Detective Inspector wanted me to tell someone, half responsible, in order that he could spread the word that, although we were trying to do our best, we are struggling unless people are willing to come forward and give evidence.'

Referring to the sheet of paper that he had taken from his jacket pocket McEvoy began to read from it.

'The big, tall West Indian with the ring through his nose is called Trax. He has a nasty sidekick called Mooch. There is also a gang called Muslim Patrol who meet up with Trax and his mate. They are mainly Muslim, and their leader is a Pakistani called Saf. Their specialty is thieving and drugs. And then there is the Albanian crew, whose specialty is using knives. They also steal cars and motor bikes and generally ride about on scooters. I'm sorry for what you've been through. As I said, Detective Inspector Marker was quite keen that I told you what the score was. If it was down to me.' McEvoy hesitated and continued, 'Maybe I'd better not say what I would do. Let's just leave it there. Just be careful Mr. Oxford.'

Shocked by what he had just heard, Albert left the vehicle to continue his walk home. Completely astounded by McEvoy's information, Albert realised that this was probably the situation up and down the country in cities and towns. Not all of it would be down to police cuts although that certainly did not help the situation. Uncontrolled immigration, including illegal immigration, was adding to the onerous burden already placed on the NHS, overworked GP's, housing and education, but there also appeared to be a complete breakdown in human relationships. Albert was quite ashamed to admit that he didn't even know, or speak, to the Somalian family three doors down from his own front door. What a state the country was in.

8.

Sunday arrived. The first Sunday without Buddy to walk around the park. At the appointed hour of opening time Albert walked to the Princess Victoria. Lech followed him through the door ten minutes later. With their pints, they sat at a table in the corner away from the fire. Albert told Lech everything that McEvoy had told him.

'So we are on our own, Albert. If the Police can do nothing, then we do something. They kill your dog. They spit at my wife. They attack my van. They put you in the hospital and that is only us. Just think about what they do to other people.'

Albert remained silent. His Polish friend was right. Perhaps it was time to fight back. The Army Corp's top caterer, Eddie, joined them at their table.

'Can I get you two a drink?'

Both men took up Eddie's offer and Eddie joined them at their table.

'I presume you heard about the dog?' said Eddie.

'Yes, it was the same crew who put Albert in hospital,' replied Lech.

'It was old Mo Connor's dog. The one I walk every

Sunday before I come here,' said Albert.

'That mob were in the pub two nights ago insulting Josie the barmaid,' said Eddie. 'When I came down from upstairs the big black ugly brute with the ring through his nose, told me I had to pay him protection money for the pub or he would put in every window and wreck the place. He gave me a week, until next Thursday, and told me I had to give him £250. He told me I was getting it cheap because he fancied the barmaid. He said the normal price was £300.'

Lech and Albert looked at each other.

'Something needs to be done, Albert.'

Albert nodded and both then resumed their normal Sunday bar positions where they were joined by tall, well dressed Mark who offered, and paid, for two more pints for them.

'I hear things are getting a bit tasty round here,' said Mark.

'How would you know that, Mark? I didn't think you were from around here.' Mark touched the side of his nose twice and said,

'Jungle drums.'

Albert returned home after devouring some of Eddie's free offerings and thought about the mood of his good friend Lech. Although trying his utmost to resist Lech's taste for revenge he couldn't help thinking that by standing up to the lowlifes was certainly one way of fighting back. Any action would have to be of such a nature that it left a meaningful message, not just on the leader, but on the rest of his gang. Other gangs in the area would hopefully get the message.

Sleep that night came in fits and starts and was punctuated by visions of various ideas of revenge. Uppermost in Albert's thought processes was the need for the message to be forceful.

9.

Monday dawned. Although the bruising and ribs were improving, Albert found it too easy to avoid taking out the taxi. His day was filled with contemplation and brooding about what had happened during the last two or three weeks. Monday evening, of course, was his trip round to the club with next door neighbour, Harry, to watch the football on satellite television. Harry had been a neighbour of Alberts for over 25 years. He had been a loyal and trusted friend and drinking companion. If Albert needed any repair work on the house, Harry was there to fix it.

On his way round to the club Albert told Harry his thoughts on the local problems and in particular the scumbags making everybody's life a misery.

'If you need any help, Albert, I would be only too willing to help. I'll never forget that bastard insulting my daughter Jane after she came to visit us. As she was getting back into her car, the nose-ring called her a slag. As she went to drive off he banged her wing mirror which smashed. She didn't hang about and it wasn't until a week later that she told me about it. I can tell you now that it was the big bastard who gave me this scar. I want to return the favour.'

'How did you get the scar, Harry?' asked Albert.

'I went to have a go at him, but I was half-pissed and he knocked me over. I gashed my face on a wall which I had fallen onto. Anyway, I don't want to say any more about it, but I've got it stored in the memory bank. As far as I'm concerned, it's unfinished business. His day will come.'

'Hopefully sooner rather than later,' replied Albert.

The Monday football game was pretty boring and after the game Albert and Harry returned to their home addresses. Passing Lech's house, he saw the giant Pole cleaning his van in the side street beside his house.

'Lech, I think I need to speak to you. Harry here, is of the same mind as us and Eddie from the pub wants to get involved. Eddie has had the bastard round the pub demanding money'

'You all come here tomorrow night. And then we talk.'

Albert knew that Eddie didn't work Tuesday evenings, so arrangements were made to meet at Lech's house at eight o' clock. Albert was tasked to inform Eddie and to take him to the meeting.

The following evening the four musketeers were sitting in Lech's living room, filling their faces with sandwiches supplied by Lech's wife Annelka. After Annelka had removed herself to the back room the four men imbibed generous amounts of Krupnik supplied by the host.

Over the course of the next four hours a vigorous discussion took place. Various plans were proposed with everyone contributing to what they thought was a reasonable solution to the problems that Trax and his gang presented to the area.

As the drink flowed the on-going discussion became quite heated and animated. Quite a few of the contributions were made with a vicious intonation, but at the end of it all the four men were in agreement with the audacious plan they had hatched. Albert had told the group the information that had unofficially been passed to him by DC McEvoy. This information had the effect of making the group more determined in their efforts. Great emphasis was mutually placed on each of them to maintain a strict secrecy over what they had in mind.

The first part of the plan was to attempt to track and monitor the regular movements of Trax. Albert thought that this was part of the fightback. The next few weeks would show whether or not they had been successful.

Eddie's final contribution was to say, 'When I was in the Middle East, we were told that if you cut the head off the monster, then the rest of the body would die.'

The other three smiled but made no comment. Albert thought to himself that what Eddie had said was probably quite near the truth.

In the following week Albert and Harry sat in Harry's old banger of a Ford Escort. They positioned themselves on the far side of the park and had for their assistance a pair of night vision binoculars which Eddie had purloined from the Army.

'I wonder how these binoculars would have helped Eddie in making soup and sandwiches in the barracks at Aldershot?' said Albert.

Harry replied, 'I don't know how he got them, and I don't really care. All I know is they are bloody useful.'

With the use of the binoculars from a safe distance, Harry and Albert were able to establish over the course of the next couple of nights a very rough pattern of movement and activity.

Even to the uninitiated, it was obvious that in the dark recesses of the park below the big horse chestnut trees, Trax and two of his lieutenants were dealing in drugs.

Various hooded, dark shapes would slink and shuffle into the park by the entrance at the western end of the park. An exchange would take place between dealer and buyer and these negotiations would continue until about midnight. Trax would then slope off, presumably heading for wherever he slept.

Harry and Albert thought it would be too unsafe to follow him all the way home, but they tailed him for a few streets from a safe distance, attempting to establish a pattern.

The following Sunday at the Princess Victoria, Albert updated Eddie and Lech. Eddie said he had paid a member of Trax's gang the £250 that Trax had asked for.

'I thought it best to pay and not upset the applecart and possibly spoil any of the plans we hope to execute.'

Both men nodded in agreement and Albert was about to continue the process of updating the other two when Mark walked into the pub and came over to join them. Albert immediately changed the subject and started complaining bitterly about the referee in yesterday's football match involving his team.

'It's funny how whenever your team loses Albert, it's always the ref's fault.'

Albert smiled, 'It only happens with this particular referee.'

After his obligatory two pints Mark left. 'He's not a great conversationalist,' said Eddie, 'I'm never quite comfortable in his company, I don't know what it is.'

In the absence of Mark, Albert, Lech and Eddie sat themselves at a table in the corner well away from the fire and other customers.

'I hear our friend with the nose jewellery gave an old boy a slap through the week just cos he got in his way on the pavement,' said Eddie.

'There is no reason why we can't put our plan into operation, soon, is there?' Lech asked.

'I will have to do some shopping this week.' said Albert. 'But yes, I agree, the sooner the better. Are you happy with everything Eddie?'

'Can't wait.' said Eddie. 'It'll take me back to all those memories in Afghanistan.'

Albert rolled his eyes and suppressed a laugh and placed his arm round Eddie's broad shoulders.

10.

Marcia didn't enjoy her work, but it was a necessity if she wanted to keep her family together. She was a 16 years old black girl with no father that she knew of. She lived at home with her mum and two younger brothers in a repressed area of north east London.

Having left school with no qualifications she now worked all the hours she could at a McDonalds on a main street in Tottenham. The money she earned went into the household and helped to keep her younger brothers in food and school uniforms.

None of the customers could be described as regulars although the premises were sometimes occupied by young black youths dressed in the uniform of the modern youth. Expensive trainers, designer jeans, a hoodie drawn up to conceal most of their face. Their conversation was held in monosyllabic grunts and whispers.

The favoured form of transport was left abandoned on the pavement outside the shop. Young mothers with prams and all other pedestrians had to negotiate a tortuous route round the bicycles littering the footway. At least these regulars did not take up much of Marcia's time, as rarely was anything bought in the restaurant.

Marcia's work consisted mainly of serving customers, either at the vehicle drive-through window, or serving walk-up customers. Not all customers would take the burgers and other assorted fast foods away from the premises. Some would stay and take advantage of the formica-topped tables and hard plastic chairs to eat their purchases. Toilets at the rear of the premises were used by customers as well as passers-by with an urgency to use the facilities.

The shop manager was Pedro, a young man of Spanish extraction. Pedro was completely disinterested in the job but saw it as a steppingstone to better things as the term 'manager' would look better on his CV. Or so he thought.

Just after the lunchtime rush, Pedro asked Marcia to clean the tables and to make sure that there was no unnecessary litter lying outside the shop in the form of cardboard cartons and plastic drink-cups and straws.

One of the tables just inside the door was occupied by three of the hoodies. Marcia cleaned their table whilst being grunted at by one of the youths. As she moved away to look outside, two hooded youths wearing scarves over their faces and crash helmets on their heads burst past her into the shop.

They both approached the table where the hooded youths were sitting. Marcia looked on with horror as the taller of the two crash-helmeted youths produced a handgun, and before any of the hoodies had a chance to move, the taller assailant raised his firearm and shot the nearest of the seated youths in his neck at point blank range. People screamed and ducked for cover. Pedro ran to the toilets.

Marcia then saw everything in slow motion. She was aware that the crash helmets were attempting to leave the shop, but transfixed, she just stood her ground blocking their way out of McDonalds.

The last thing Marcia ever saw was the gun being raised to her head, a blinding flash, and then, nothing. Just blackness.

Pedro Albertez poked his head out of one of the cubicles in the ladies toilets. A large West Indian woman looked at him and said, 'It's alright big brave man, all de trouble is over. You can use de men's restroom now.'

Sheepishly, Pedro made his way back into the customer section of the fast-food shop.

The lifeless body of young Marcia lay sprawled on the floor with her body at a grotesque angle. A pool of bright red blood circled her head on the flooring. The body of a young black male lay slumped on the table nearest the street door. Blood, from a messy neck wound, had spilled onto the table and dripped down onto the floor.

All the customers who had been in the shop had long since fled, apart from the large West Indian lady who came out from the toilet area, picked up her order from the unattended counter, and left the shop, shaking her head.

Pedro Albertez was informed by his young deputy manager that the police and ambulance emergency services had been called. Pedro hoped that all of this would not reflect badly on his CV.

Within three minutes a paramedic arrived on a motor-

50

bike and very quickly established that both Marcia and the young black male were deceased.

A loud screech of brakes heralded the arrival of uniform police officers.

The officers were not surprised to hear that there were no witnesses and no descriptions. They had heard it all before. Nobody wanted to get involved.

Tottenham Mercury

Yesterday, at a fast-food outlet in Tottenham High Road, two young people were shot dead at point blank range. One of the victims was a young black girl aged 16 years who cannot be named at the moment for legal reasons. Police are appealing for witnesses...

11.

The following day Albert trudged through the rain to Ray's terraced house. The shiny London taxi was waiting for him. Albert thought about all those rain-soaked customers who would be desperate to seek shelter from the incessant rain.

'A good day for working the cab, Albert. This weather is God's gift to taxi drivers.'

Albert didn't have the heart to tell Ray that he wouldn't be picking up any customers that day but had more important business to attend to than plying for hire on the capital's streets.

Albert had removed enough cash from his floor-safe to pay for his shopping expedition. Then, using his know-ledge of the maze that formed London's thoroughfares, Albert drove to the carefully selected hardware shop near the South Circular Road.

Albert spent some time carefully choosing his purchases. The items were then placed onto a wide supermarket trolley. After loading the items he required, he went to the till and paid cash. Albert enlisted the help of the young assistant to push the wide trolley out through the rear door to the car park where, to his relief, the rain had stopped. It took Albert fifteen minutes to load his purchases into the rear section of the cab.

Albert phoned the Princess Victoria and informed Eddie that, even allowing for heavy traffic, he would be at the pub in just over an hour.

'I'll be ready for you. Park near the gate to the pub garden and ring me when you're there.'

Just over an hour later Albert was parked outside the pub. The front entrance door to the pub was on the main road and the garden entrance was just round the corner in an adjoining side street. The garden gate was over eight feet tall with two wooden stout panels which swung shut and was secured by a heavy-duty padlock. During the summer months it was another means of access to the pub and customers, many with dogs, would avail themselves of the garden furniture in what could only be loosely described as a garden. But, at this time of the year in the winter months the gate remained closed except when there was a delivery from the brewery. On these occasions Eddie would open up and the draymen would lower kegs of bitter and lager through a nine-foot-wide hatchway directly into Eddie's cellar.

Albert rang Eddie inside the building. Albert saw the gates swing open and Eddie's beaming smile welcomed Albert and the taxi into the garden courtyard. Eddie asked Albert to wait whilst he closed the garden gates behind Albert.

Eddie retired back inside the pub and his head and shoulders suddenly appeared from the cellar after he had opened the cellar flaps.

'Ok, Albert, you can start unloading the gear and I will stow it down here. We can have a look through it later.'

The purchases were lowered into the cellar by placing them on a large open dumb waiter which was then winched down manually by using a crank and lever. After twenty minutes of hard graft, the load was secured in a cleared space in the cellar well away from barrels, tubing and crates containing alcoholic bottled drinks and bottled soft drinks. The lighting was provided by a single bulb with flex hanging from a beamed ceiling.

That evening Albert met up with Lech and Harry in the saloon bar and after one obligatory pint supplied by Eddie, the three men were escorted behind the bar and out into the living accommodation area of the pub.

A carpeted staircase led to the living quarters of Eddie and his wife. A woman who was rarely seen, Eddie's wife contented herself with reading a glut of glossy magazines whilst occasionally glancing at a saved collection of recorded television soap operas and a plethora of old black and white films starring famous faces from the distant past. Her contribution to running the public house was to prepare the food that was sold and served downstairs.

Built into the recess below the stairs was a door which, when opened, led to a flight of metal stairs which eventually led down into the roomy cellar by use of a metal handrail. A light switch at the top of this staircase led to the room being lit when switched on.

A substantial mound of goods, which was the subject of

Albert's shopping expedition, lay on top of four pallets in the cleared area on the far side of the cellar.

'I wore gloves today,' said Albert, 'and Eddie wore gloves earlier when we unloaded,' Albert informed the other two. 'It's absolutely vital that whatever we do from now on we have to wear a pair of these.'

Albert picked up a box containing light blue latex gloves. He issued his two companions with a pair of gloves and they set about examining Albert's purchases.

They spent an hour poring over the equipment and after disposing of their gloves in a deputed rubbish bag, they retired to the bar. The examination had been conducted with an air of near silence and maximum seriousness.

Lech was pleased that everyone was focused. Uppermost in Lech's mind was the image of that poor dog hanging from a tree.

12.

The following day Lech was up early as usual. After grabbing a quick slice of toast he went out to fulfil his commitment to clean an estate agent's office after the office had undergone a major refurbishment.

Missing out on lunch, Lech worked on till just past four o'clock in the afternoon. He then rang his wife Annelka to say that there was a problem with the van and that after he had finished he would drop it off at his local repair garage for them to sort out the problem. Lech then rang Eddie to tell him to be prepared to open the pub garden gates in about fifteen minutes' time.

As Lech approached the pub Eddie had the gates already open. Lech drove the van into the yard and parked near the cellar hatchway. Eddie closed the garden gates and then went to open the cellar hatchway.

Lech opened the side door of the van. He started to unload his cleaning materials. He handed these to Eddie, who, by this time, was already in the cellar waiting to receive the various items of cleaning equipment.

Lech was pleased to see Eddie wearing a pair of latex gloves. Lech joined Eddie in the cellar and, donning a pair of the light blue gloves, he proceeded to examine the purchases made by Albert. Carefully selecting what he wanted with Eddie's assistance, he begun to load a flat wooden dumb waiter which was normally used to raise and lower barrels and crates to and from the cellar. The dumb waiter was operated by a lever and handle just below the open space of the hatchway.

Back in the garden area just by the hatchway, Lech entered by the side door of his van and closed himself in by shutting the sliding door. He worked by the interior light of the van.

The rear cabin of the van was completely empty. He started unwrapping lengths of heavy-duty black plastic sheeting. He examined the rolls of gaffer tape, a large pair of scissors and reels of thick twine. He was also assisted by the light of a powerful manual lamp, and Lech commenced his work.

He toiled away for the next hour and whilst grafting, Lech reflected on his situation. Entering the UK some thirty years ago as a ten-year-old boy with his Polish parents, he had struggled to adapt to life in his new homeland. He did not speak English and he found school very difficult but, with the help of an English teacher, and by staying after school for extra lessons, he mastered the complexities of the English language without becoming an expert.

When reaching the age of fifteen, Lech left school and worked for a cleaning business based in Wapping. The pay was poor, but Lech was happy that he had some financial independence from his parents and on occasions he would visit a Polish cafe in Hackney where he took a fancy to the waitress, a young lady called Annelka, who was also of Polish extraction. Annelka had been born in the UK but her parents originated from a village in Poland about 30 miles from the town where Lech had been brought up.

A romance ensued, inevitably followed by a wedding. Financial circumstances were very poor and living with Annelka's parents in Hackney meant that life was difficult, but nevertheless, the couple were happy in each other's company.

The couple's aim was to start a family, but Lech decided that his income had to increase. He decided to set up his own cleaning business. He managed to secure a loan from his father which would pay for transport, advertising cards, cleaning materials and in a bold, but controversial move, he adopted some of his former employers' customers. Before long the business had established itself allowing Lech and Annelka to move into their small house near the park.

Fate was not kind to the Polish couple, however, as it was discovered that Annelka was unable to bear a child. This was a bitter blow to both, and it was during this time that Lech made more use of the local hostelries and whilst drinking in the Princess Victoria he met, amongst others, Albert. A strong friendship developed, mainly featuring their occupancy of the saloon bar, but both would be visitors in each other's houses.

Lizzie, Albert's late wife, would revel in stories about Poland and Annelka was similarly enchanted by Albert's tales of the London taxi trade. Annelka and Lech became very close and supportive to Albert when Lizzie became ill and finally succumbed to her illness.

Having lived in the area for some years Lech was aware of the gang culture that operated in the park near his address. He had had dealings with the ugly brute called Trax before and held him responsible for the damage to his van, his dustbin being set alight, and the insults directed at his wife. But more than anything he was incensed that anybody could do such a thing to an innocent, friendly dog and he felt for his friend Albert who had suffered mentally for the last couple of years after the death of his wife.

Whilst working in the back of the van Lech wondered about the other two intended participants in their plan. He obviously knew Eddie from the Princess Victoria but regarded Eddie as a figure of fun and joviality. Eddie was teased mercilessly by Albert, Lech and others, about his Army career, with Eddie insisting that he saw active service and wasn't just confined to the kitchens of the Army Catering Corps. Nevertheless, Eddie was good, solid company, a genial host and had obviously been upset by the demand of money from this gang leader. Eddie had also despaired of how his little area of London had descended into a cesspit of immorality and thuggery, brought on by uncontrolled gangs operating as they pleased.

Eddie had volunteered himself without hesitation and had already demonstrated a willingness to organise and develop the plan by offering the facilities of the public house for the covert work that Lech was now undertaking.

With regard to Albert's next-door neighbour, Harry, Lech knew there was a strong bond between Albert and

Harry. They had been friends for a number of years, social-ised together, and when Lizzie was alive, they would be in each other's houses drinking, eating and sharing a laugh.

As for this type of adventure and what was proposed, Lech had a nagging doubt in his mind as to whether Albert was up to the task and whether he would have the stomach for the plan they intended to execute. He had no doubts about Harry's ability to cause mayhem. Time would tell.

Lech's labours took slightly longer than he expected but on completion, he parked his vehicle in a corner of the yard and knocked on the back door of the pub. Once inside the saloon bar Lech was pleased to see both Albert and Harry with a pint of beer in front of them.

'All done?' asked Albert.

'Yes, all done and no problems. Good to go. What are you two doing here tonight? This is not your usual habit.'

'A young fifteen-year-old girl was attacked this afternoon just after it got dark. She was bashed across the face and had her mobile and purse stolen. Everybody knows who it was. The brute and his Asian mate, but nobody wants to get involved. The Old Bill has been informed but nobody wants to know,' said Harry, his face getting redder by the second. 'I'm pleased we are doing what we are. It can't happen soon enough, in my opinion.'

'I'll drink to that,' said Eddie and ordered four more pints from the bar.

13.

The following day would be pivotal, thought Harry. The day was miserable, with sleeting rain and a strong wind. Harry hoped that the weather would clear as if the present conditions persisted, there was a chance Trax would not show up later. Now happily retired after working for over 30 years at Smithfield meat market, Harry spent his days, either in the garden, or in some hostelry.

Once a week he would travel by the Central line to St Paul's underground station and walk round to the meat market. One of the many focal points of the market was the Cock public house, situated right in the middle of the market, and it was here that Harry would meet up with his old workmates and enjoy their ribald sense of humour and storytelling. Invariably, Harry would eventually leave for home with a parcel of meat for later consumption.

Next door Albert sat in his armchair contemplating their plans. Suddenly, his mobile phone rang. A withheld number. Normally Albert didn't give succour to equity call chancers, PPI merchants or scammers, but for some reason decided to answer it.

'Meet me at the junction of Stair Street and Berkeley in

twenty minutes.'

Albert thought he vaguely recognised the voice and was perplexed as to why a mystery caller would want to meet up with him.

Albert donned his coat and walked towards the intended venue, vowing to himself to be ultra-careful and to scout the area beforehand. But on the way a familiar car drew alongside him, and a similarly familiar voice said, 'Get in, Mr. Oxford.'

The familiar voice belonged to DC McEvoy. Albert sat in the front passenger seat.

'Mr. Oxford, once again I'm speaking to you in a completely unofficial capacity. This little meeting of ours is not taking place. I have to tell you that you should tread very carefully. It has come to the notice of my governor that you are making yourself busy with Trax and his gang. You need to be very careful.'

'Why are you telling me this, Mr. McEvoy?'

'You and your mates are nice blokes. You don't need to get involved in this,' he replied.

'You told me the police are powerless, your resources stretched to breaking point and this mob is running wild, petrifying the community. Law and order has broken down. Can you see why some decent people are a bit upset?'

'Be careful!' was McEvoy's parting shot before opening the car door, allowing Albert to exit and return home.

On the walk home Albert mulled over his conversation with the young detective. McEvoy wouldn't be warning Albert of his own volition. It was pretty clear that the information had been passed down from higher up the chain of Police Command. But, from how high? And was McEvoy telling him to be aware because he knew what was going on but stopped short of forbidding Albert and his accomplices from taking further direct action. Albert decided he would not tell his crew as he didn't want to spook any of them into making a rash decision.

14.

Later that evening, Albert and Harry drove to the Princess Victoria. Albert collected a large canvas bag from Eddie whilst Harry picked up a large box from the cellar and they then drove to the far side of the park in Harry's old Escort. The box and canvas bag were safely stowed in the boot. The weather had relented and as they sat quietly, they were both relieved to see that the drug dealing business in the park continued as usual.

Once that had been established they drove back to Lech's house, where they dropped off the canvas bag and box into the kitchen of Lech's house. Harry and Albert returned Harry's car and drove to their own street, parked it, and both then walked back to Lech's house.

'All set to go, Lech, he's in the park,' said Harry. 'Time to put our plan into operation.' There then followed an awkward group hug. Albert rang Eddie and said,

'All systems go, Eddie.'

'I'll be ready, good luck,' he replied.

As Annelka was visiting her mother, the house belonged to the three of them. The contents of the canvas bag were emptied onto the kitchen floor. The pile included three blue cotton boiler suits which had been carefully selected as two sizes too big for each of them so that they could be worn over the clothes they were wearing.

Each of them dressed in silence and all made sure that a pair of the blue plastic gloves had been donned. Brand new black training shoes replaced the footwear they had on and their outfit was completed by each of them stuffing a black woollen balaclava into the trouser pocket of the boiler suit. Handing the keys of his cleaner's van to Albert, they silently left Lech's house.

Because of the time of evening and prevailing cold conditions there was no one on the streets. Albert clicked open the van and Lech and Harry clambered into the back of the van through the sliding side door while Albert climbed into the driver's seat and switched on the ignition. Albert carefully drove to the predetermined spot where it was intended they would lay in wait for their prey.

In the back of the van, Harry was agog with how the rear of the van had been transformed. Covering every square inch of space was black plastic sheeting, secured by heavy duty tape. Even the roof of the van had been sealed. Both men sat on the floor of the van and sat in silence as Albert drove the van slowly to the location.

The location had been carefully selected. Of primary importance was the fact that it was on Trax's route home, or to wherever he usually headed after dealing.

The site was also in a street, free of CCTV cameras, and contained houses and small front gardens down one side of the street. Trax's habit was to walk down the side of the road in which the houses were situated. It was thought that this was probably to allow him to look into cars parked there and to ascertain if there was anything worth stealing from the motor vehicles.

Albert had parked the van facing the way Trax would walk so Albert had his eyes firmly set on the rear-view mirror waiting for the beast to appear in shot. Sitting in the dark, the time stretched out and seemed to go on, interminably. There was no movement from the rear of the vehicle.

Although dark, Albert was confident that he would be able to spot Trax two hundred and fifty yards down the road. Albert looked at the houses to his left. Most were in darkness with curtains drawn but at one house he thought he noticed the flick of a net curtain being replaced. Probably some nosey parker wondering why there was a strange van in their street.

In the back of the van, Lech and Harry sat in silence. It was pitch black. Very occasionally Lech flicked on a small pencil beam flashlight just to ensure that he knew the exact position of the handle that would allow him to get out of the van at a second's notice.

The street was quiet, no one was about, and the only noise Albert could hear was his own breathing.

Suddenly he saw Trax in the passenger rear view mirror. After two quick taps from Albert from the front portion of the van, Albert saw in his rear-view mirror, the side door of the van slide backwards with barely a sound.

In the same mirror he saw the dark clad figure of Harry slip into the front garden of the house next to the van. Harry had the cover of an overgrown hedgerow aa he lay in wait for their intended prey. Harry pulled on his balaclava.

The target appeared to be talking on his mobile phone as he walked slowly in the direction of the van.

As he drew level with the van, he realised that the side door of the van was open. He went to peer inside but before he could react, he was hit by a rugby tackle coming from the direction of the hedge. The two shapes were propelled by the force of the tackle towards the open door of the van.

At that moment the large frame of Lech grabbed Trax and almost immediately, rendered Trax unconscious with a blow to his head using a small club hammer.

Albert quickly left the driver's cab and ran to the nearside of the van. He scooped up Trax's mobile and threw it into the back of the van. He saw that Trax had been rendered unconscious. Albert quietly closed the sliding door of the van.

Lech and Harry were now engaged in the process of securing and immobilising Trax by using plastic cable ties as handcuffs and tape to seal off his mouth. His legs were bound together.

Albert returned to the driver's seat and turned the key in the ignition and started the engine. Before he moved off, Albert texted Eddie with the words, '*Aboard*.'

Carefully, and almost too slowly, Albert began to drive towards the Princess Victoria. The streets at this late hour of the night were deserted, with the locals tucked up in the warmth of their homes.

In the rear of the van Trax was still unconscious but appeared to be breathing normally. There was no immediate sign that consciousness was being regained, but there was a visible large contusion by his left ear which extended across his left cheekbone towards his huge ringed nose.

As Albert slowly approached The Princess Victoria, he was pleased to see the rotund shape of Eddie standing by the rear gates of the garden area. The gates were already open and Albert carefully drove the van through into the yard area and then was pleased to see that the flaps to the cellar had also been pulled open revealing a low light in the cellar area. Albert carefully parked the van with the sliding door of the van adjacent to the opening of the cellar.

Albert quickly went to the sliding door and pulled it back. He was impressed by what he saw. Trax had been bound hand and foot and, with the liberal use of tape, resembled an Egyptian mummy. A gap in the tape around his head revealed that Trax was now conscious and his big eyes were wide open and agog with terror, darting back and forth between the four men.

Lech and Harry pulled him from the van and in a swift movement they lifted the bound body towards the entrance to the cellar. The taped-up body of Trax was laid next to the opening of the cellar. Employing his boot, Harry rolled the body towards the opening. Trax crashed onto the concrete floor of the cellar with a dull thud. Albert closed the sliding door of the van and Eddie closed the cellar door flaps.

All four men now entered through the back door of the pub, which by now, was empty of all customers. They descended the stairs down into the cellar where Albert could just about make out the groans of pain coming from the distorted body shape that was Trax. Above them, the pub was eerily quiet, the regulars having long since left for their respective homes, happily intoxicated.

Josie, the barmaid, had already cleared up the dirty glasses and washed them. Tables had been wiped and rearranged into the set positions round the tables ready for the next day's business. Josie had left for home by the front door of the pub, locking it behind her as was her usual custom.

There was no conversation between the four men, but Albert felt a glow of satisfaction at the execution of a plan that had appeared to run like clockwork, so far.

The cellar had been transformed by Eddie. The area below the cellar flaps, and onto which Trax had been dropped, was now extensively covered with sheets of the heavy-duty plastic. The empty barrels and crates of soft drinks and mixers had been repositioned in the cellar onto wooden pallets leaving a large expanse of floor, covered by the plastic sheeting. To the side of this cleared space lay a pile of Albert's purchases still to be used.

Trax appeared to be extremely agitated judging by his eye movement. Lech approached him and whispered,

'This is for all the damage you've caused me, for insulting my wife and my neighbours.'

He then picked up a tyre lever and struck Trax on his ankle with such force that it was obvious to all the spectators that the ankle bone had been smashed. The eyes got wider and movement was not possible due to the bindings. Next up was Eddie who had a large pair of pliers in his hand.

'Your big mistake with me was that you demanded money from me. You are a fucking thug who doesn't deserve to breathe the same air as us. You have insulted me, and my staff, and I always promised myself that one day I would get even with you.'

At that, Harry secured Trax's right hand and with the pliers and an audible crack, Eddie proceeded to break every one of the fingers of Trax's right hand.

Trax looked like he was going to pass out but Harry stepped in and said,

'I'm not going to hurt you but I will be the one who disposes of your carcass. Nothing personal, really, but you shouldn't have messed with me or my family or my neighbourhood. I've lived here for years and we've just had enough. You and your type are vermin, scum of the earth, and this place will be all the better without you and your fucking pals. It's been long overdue that the people of his area have had to fight back against your type.'

Albert stepped into the gap in front of Trax which had been vacated by Harry.

'Do you realise what you have fucking done? Four middle aged blokes, plodding along in life's slow lane, minding their own business. You come along, terrorising good ordinary people, making their lives a misery. But do you know what did it with me? Not only did you kill an innocent dog, a lovable, innocent animal, but you crudely strung the poor bastard up from a tree to try to impress me that you could do anything you like, and that you didn't fear anyone. Well, your time has come, you are breathing your last breaths of oxygen. You are going to be dispatched to your maker. You will not be missed by anyone because you are a useless lump of shit. Your body will never be found. This is for Buddy, and in case you didn't know it, that was the name of that lovely dog.'

Those were the last words Trax heard as Albert smashed a tyre lever into the head of Trax. After five whacks it was apparent that Trax could no longer be alive. Eddie's Army First Aid course allowed him to establish that there was no pulse. Job done!

There then followed a small congratulatory pat on the back from each and Harry said, 'There's a bit of tidying up to be done. We mustn't spoil anything now by being careless. Everybody knows what they've got to do.'

Lech left the basement and returned to the van still wearing his boiler suit. He had removed his balaclava but was still wearing the nylon gloves. With two empty hold-alls he had taken from the cellar, he went to his van where he completely stripped out all plastic sheeting and tape. He also picked up the mobile phone Trax had been using and removed the sim card. He placed everything in the canvas holdall and returned to the cellar.

In the meantime, the other three men had not been idle. The lifeless body of Trax had been enveloped in folds and re-folds of the heavy-duty plastic sheeting and lay in state in its own space in a clear portion of the concrete flooring.

To clean the cellar in normal circumstances Eddie would use a hose attached to a standpipe and tap and he would use these at least once a week to wash away beer and other spillages. This water would flow into a shallow gully and drain, set in the concrete floor.

Returning to the cellar Lech could see that Eddie had done an excellent job of cleaning the floor space and everything looked back to normal apart from the corpse lying on the floor. Disrobing out of his boiler suit, Lech placed the boiler suit and balaclava in a neat pile on the floor. Before removing his gloves, he took everything out of the canvas bags and placed them on the pile. He then removed his gloves and threw them onto the mound.

Albert and Harry also took off their boiler suits and placed these, along with the balaclavas and gloves, onto the growing pile of discarded equipment. Eddie discarded his gloves.

'I don't suppose there's a chance of a quick pint before finding our way home, is there Eddie?' said Harry, 'thirsty work.'

All four laughed and within ten minutes they sat in silence in the dark in the saloon bar nursing a pint.

'His mobile phone has gone onto the rubbish but I removed this first,' whispered Lech, producing the sim card from the phone. 'I think they can trace them so we don't want it here or near the body.'

'I'll take care of that,' said Albert. 'I'll make sure that it doesn't compromise any of us.' Albert placed the sim card in his pocket. Finishing their respective drinks, Eddie ushered the three others out through the rear door. Lech got into his van and offered the other two a lift but they both declined, settling instead for a walk home in the crispness of the night, in an attempt to clear their heads of that evening's tumultuous activities.

Eddie silently reopened the rear gate to the courtyard

and Lech and his van disappeared into the frostiness.

Albert and Harry walked in silence to their homes. The silence was broken by Albert who said,

'I'm going to get rid of this sim card.' As he said this, he wiped the sim card on his sleeve and then slipped into a street drain.

'What time tomorrow, Harry?' asked Albert.

'I don't think I'll be able to sleep much, Albert, so we can be as early as you want.'

'Tennish?' asked Albert. A nod from Harry confirmed this.

Lying in bed, Albert could hear a cacophony of sirens and wild foxes and smiled at the thought of the noises, all celebrating the demise of a wretch. Albert slept soundly.

15.

Just after ten o'clock the following morning, Harry knocked on Albert's door. Harry had a heavy-looking bag with him.

'What have you told your missus, Harry?'

'Nothing.' said Harry, 'She has gone to visit her sister in Southend. She will be away all day. She did ask why I was late last night but I told her that you and I had got the flavour and got a little bit pissed. She still made me breakfast, though, which means that she's ok about it. I had a good breakfast because of what lies in front of us. I am going to take the car round to the pub because this bag weighs a ton.'

The two men then drove to the pub in the Escort and entered the pub using the main front door. Eddie greeted them and Albert saw that the pub, at this early hour, was empty. Eddie led the pair of them to the head of the stairs, opened the cellar door, and said,

'When you need food or drinks, just let me know. There's a private toilet for my use here at the top of the stairs so you don't need to go into the bar and get clocked by any nosey parkers.'

Albert and Harry, who was carrying his heavy bag, descended the stairs and switched on the single light bulb. The place was as it was in the middle of the night. First things first, thought Albert, was to make sure they were suitably clothed.

From one of his shopping-trip bags he took two pairs of polypropylene disposable suits as used by police forensic staff. Both suits had a hood and were elasticated at the cuffs and ankles. Harry placed on his head a pair of plastic goggles and both men donned another pair of clean plastic gloves.

Harry produced from his canvas bag his old tools of the trade which he had used whilst gainfully employed at Smithfield Meat Market. These included a cleaver, a bone-saw, blades, pliers and a variety of lethal-looking knives.

Albert knew what was going to happen and was not looking forward to what lay in store. He was, however, prepared to assist his big friend in whatever needed to be done.

Albert had his own part to play, and for this he prepared himself for his role in the proceedings by laying out a pile of plastic sheeting cut into six foot by six-foot squares. Alongside, he had the obligatory roll of gaffer tape, sharp scissors and knives.

Harry set about his work. First, the body had to be unwrapped. The sheeting was used to supplement the plastic covering that had already been laid out. As rigor mortis had begun to wear off, it was relatively easy to remove the tape and the next job was to remove the clothing of the big lump who lay prostrate on the stone-cold floor. As Harry removed the tracksuit bottoms he retrieved a package of little paper screws which Albert thought would contain the drugs that were touted to lost and needy souls. Harry flushed these packets down the drain. Harry also removed a roll of banknotes and threw the roll, bound with an elastic band, across the room to Albert.

'That should help to pay off the national debt, for all the gear you have had to buy.'

Although Albert had been prepared to pay for his purchases out of cash he had lying in his floor safe at home, he took the bankroll. Money which had been earned in the taxi, and not all of it declared to Her Majesty's Revenue and Customs, had been kept for a rainy day. The money would replace the amount he had paid out.

Once the body had been stripped, the clothes were placed in the mound of items to be disposed of. It was obvious to Albert that Harry was going to start his operations from the top when he took hold of his bone saw.

'Before you do that, Harry, can you separate his nose ring from his nose? I wouldn't mind it as a memento.'

'No problem, mate,' said Harry, with a quizzical look.

With that Harry skilfully sliced the ring from the large nostril and handed it to Albert who carefully cleaned it and placed it in his trouser pocket below his plastic overall. Albert looked away as Harry used the bone-saw to sever the head of Trax away from the body. The noise of the chopping and slicing unnerved Albert but he was determined to be as stoic as the circumstances would allow.

Surprisingly, there was not as much blood as Albert thought there would be. Harry had told him that after death, blood pools into the interstitial tissues of the body. This occurs six to twelve hours after death.

'All yours, Albert,' Harry said, pointing to the severed head. Albert took hold of the head. He couldn't believe how heavy it was. He placed it on the first of the plastic sheets and wrapped it carefully, securing the package with the heavy-duty tape.

Albert felt better now that the ugly head was not staring at him. For the next two hours, Harry went about his business of dismembering the body. He appeared to be quite detached and operated as if he was working on a side of beef at the meat market. The upper limbs were detached from the torso at the point of the clavicle and required a couple of hefty whacks with the biggest of the meat cleavers. Muscles and sinews were cut with a variety of knives. The arms were halved at the elbow joints, again with the use of the cleaver. The legs were separated from the torso by sawing through muscle and bone at a point near the pelvic and hip bone.

Both legs were separated at the knee with the large cleaver and by using one of the big sharp knives. The torso would present the biggest problem as Harry knew that if the torso was left intact, it would present a problem in handling and disposal.

The operation to cut the torso into quarters took a considerable time but Harry was knowledgeable as far as human anatomy was concerned. The rib cage was circumvented and the spine was severed with a couple of heavy blows with the largest of the cleavers. The only disconcerting aspect of the proceedings was the slight stench emanating from the already decomposing body.

When wrapping the body parts into their respective parcels, Albert had to ensure that the body fluids that had been contained in the body parts were available for the flushing operation which would take place at the completion of their tasks.

By mid-afternoon the tasks had been completed. On the floor of the cellar were placed differing mounds of clothing, tools and body parts, carefully wrapped in plastic. The body parts were divided into four limbs, four sections of torso, upper and lower right and left, and the head. Albert had stuck to his task gainfully but needed assistance from Harry to wrap up the parts of the torso.

Suddenly, and without warning, there were two sharp knocks on the door at the top of the cellar steps. Both men looked at each other and stopped in their tracks. Albert went to the top of the steps and slowly opened the door. There was no one there but, as Albert looked down he noticed two pints of ale. Laughing, he scooped up both and then closed the door behind him.

'A present from the Army Catering Corps. Good old Eddie. He's got his uses, bless him.'

A mound, consisting of clothing which had been used by the three men, and the clothing of Trax, lay on the edge of the operating theatre. All used gloves were also discarded onto this pile as well as the suits that the surgeons had just used. The sheeting which had been used for the dismembering operation was hosed down with the cellar hose and placed into the mound of rubbish to be discarded. Both men carefully inspected their place of work and were satisfied that the area had been forensically cleaned to the best of their ability. They both retired to the bar where Eddie greeted them with a raised eyebrow.

'All done.' whispered Harry, as the pub still had its fill of afternoon drinkers. Albert and Harry sat at an empty table in the corner. Eddie appeared with two platefuls of cheese and pickle sandwiches. Albert couldn't face his sandwich as he still had the stench of the morning's work in his nostrils. Harry had no such problems and devoured not only his own, but Albert's as well.

'What's your plan now, Albert?'

'This afternoon I've got to see a man about a boat and then I'm going home to have a kip. We've got a late night tonight. Lech has got some shopping to do today. He's going to meet us at the pub later.'

'What's Eddie got to do?' asked Harry.

'He's in charge of sandwiches and other refreshments,' smiled Albert. 'But he has to hose out the cellar to make sure that all traces of our late friend have been washed down the plug hole.'

Both men walked home together. On the way, Harry took a call from his wife.

'What a result. Libby is staying down with her sister. I won't have to lie about what I'm doing tonight.'

16.

Later that afternoon Albert travelled to Bethnal Green on the Central Line Underground. He walked to the offices of the premises in Roman Road which he had located on Google. He had an appointment with Mr Evans, a small rotund, bald man with rimless spectacles which were perched on the end of his nose.

Business was concluded quite swiftly, especially when Albert produced a wad of notes, which Trax had kindly donated to the cause. He paid the businessman for a month's rent on a canal narrowboat moored on the River Lea navigation canal. It was situated at the northwest side of a large expanse of grassy fields called Hackney Marshes.

Albert took possession of a plastic folder containing site position, operating instructions and a complete inventory. He returned home and invited Harry into his kitchen area where they both pored over the documents.

'There doesn't seem to be a problem here,' said Harry. 'We will need to make sure we have enough fuel and to find out exactly where the boat is. Are you happy about steering the thing, Albert?'

'No problem, Lizzie and I used to rent a canal boat on

the Norfolk Broads years ago. There's no waves or tide to worry about and it's just a case of steering it and sticking to the right side of the road.'

After a bite to eat, Harry and Albert drove to Lech's address just round the corner. Lech answered his doorbell and told them to drive round to the side road where his van was parked.

On their arrival Lech opened up the side door of the van and all three men proceeded to unload three heavy canvas bags onto the back seat of Harry's Escort.

'Bloody hell, these are heavy,' said Albert, when the job had been done. 'How much did you spend?'

'It doesn't matter. Look upon it as my contribution to the cause,' said Lech.

Albert shook his head and pressed a few notes into the Pole's big hand.

'A present from Trax,' said Albert.

Once the transfer of bags had been made, Harry and Albert set off for Hackney Marshes. As they pulled up in the car park Albert said to Harry, 'I'm going to walk across the Marshes and fiddle about with the boat. It will take me a bit of time to walk across there, identify the boat, make sure everything is shipshape and then take her to where we agreed. If I was you, Harry, I wouldn't be at the meeting place for another half-hour at least. No need to draw attention to ourselves unnecessarily.'

'Got that,' replied Harry and with that, Albert set off on his trek across multiple football pitches which made up most of this part of the Marshes. He was aided by a big powerful pencil light torch. Albert walked through a clearing in the trees, which flanked the River Lea Navigation Canal and made his way along the deserted tow path past a succession of canal boats and barges.

Surprisingly, quite a few were occupied, with wispy plumes of smoke emanating from thin metal chimneys. Albert occasionally heard the muffled conversations of occupants and, judging from the flickering lights inside, it appeared the various occupants were watching television.

After five minutes walking Albert spotted the Scarpa, a long thin, red and green coloured canal boat secured by rope, aft and fore, to two metal pegs hammered into the grassy bank of the towpath. Albert skipped aboard and using one of the keys, opened the door into the central compartment.

Albert found a switch and turned on the interior light and quickly established that the fuel level was at its maximum. The calor gas cylinder felt full and using his torch Albert stepped outside. The small engine room and tiller were situated at the rear of the boat and an adequate amount of deck space was still available for Albert's plans.

Moving forward past the interior cabin and the kitchen galley to the bow of the slim boat, Albert was pleased once again to see a fair bit of decking and two large tarpaulins stowed in the forward space. A couple of pot plants were placed on the low roof of the interior cabin.

Passing back through the craft, Albert passed a small toilet and examined the kitchen which contained a sink and single gas ring for cooking. Albert walked through the living area which consisted of a cushioned bench and a couple of plastic chairs.

He went to the engine room and started up the engine. After a couple of hiccups, the engine spluttered into life and a belch of black smoke emitted from the upright steel chimney.

Whilst the craft was still in neutral gear, Albert slipped off the two mooring ropes and quickly went back to the tiller. He kicked the engine into gear, and, knowing that the maximum speed of this boat was five miles per hour, he carefully manoeuvred the boat away from the grassy bank and steered on the right-hand side of the canal in a southerly direction towards the proposed meeting place with Harry.

Harry, meanwhile, had driven off the main road to Hackney and positioned himself by a small car park near the western side of the canal.

After an anxious ten-minute wait, Harry saw in the distance the red and green night lights of a canal boat moving slowly in his direction. As instructed, he greeted the sight of this boat with three flashes of his torch.

Harry was pleased to see three flashes in the distance returning his signal and he went down to the edge of the towpath to help Albert secure the canal boat. Although the waterway was lined with canal boats of differing shapes and sizes there were at least two spare pegs with which to secure Captain Albert's vessel.

Albert slowed to a stop by engaging a touch of reverse gear and using the tiller, he threw a rope to Harry who secured the forward position. Albert skipped ashore and secured the rear part of the boat.

'Well done, Albert, I must admit I was not brimming

with confidence about your nautical abilities, but you steered that in like an old pro,' said Harry.

'A life on the ocean wave,' smiled Albert. 'In a different life I would have been Admiral of the Fleet!' Harry laughed and said,

'Yeah, and Eddie would have been General Montgomery of El Alamein.'

Both men laughed and walked to the car, where on the rear seat lay the three large canvas bags containing Lech's shopping.

Although this part of the canal was overlooked by some concrete high-rise apartments, Albert was fairly sure that at this hour of the night the occupants would either be in bed or huddled around their televisions. Most of the apartments were in darkness and the remainder looked at peace with the night.

Due to the excessive weight of the three bags, Albert and Harry could only manage one bag at a time, half carrying and half dragging the bags down to the boat.

After considerable effort all three bags were eventually placed onto the bow section. Albert covered the bags with one of the tarpaulins and secured it with hooks to the side of the deck.

Once done, the two men returned to the car. Although the Princess Victoria was closed for business, Harry rang Eddie, 'We are coming to pick up some parcels. Everything went like clockwork thanks to Horatio Nelson, here.'

'I'll be waiting by the back gate. Just drive in and I will give you a hand.'

Harry drove to the pub and, true to his word, the back

gate swung open. Harry positioned the car near the flaps of the cellar which had both been opened.

Once the street gates had been closed all three men entered the pub by the rear door and descended the steps to the cellar where a number of black plastic packages lay on the floor by the manual lift. There were nine wrapped packages in all and the parcels were all placed and secured onto the dumb waiter.

Harry and Albert returned to the car in the yard and once Eddie had established that they were in a position to receive the packages, he winched the load up to ground level in the garden area.

Without wasting too much time Harry and Albert loaded the packages into the boot space of the Escort. Both removed their gloves and threw them down to Eddie who placed them on the pile of rubbish which had been earmarked for disposal the following day.

Harry got behind the wheel and watched as the cellar flaps were closed. Two minutes later Eddie appeared in the courtyard and as the Escort was driven out through the street gates, Eddie secured them and retired to the pub and to his bed.

Harry drove to the spot by the towpath where they had left the canal boat. There was an eerie silence and the only sound was created by emergency-service sirens miles away. Donning fresh gloves, both men then set about removing the packages from the boot and they took them individually to the boat where they placed the wrapped body parts in the stern of the boat and covered them with the spare tarpaulin. Once this had been achieved, Harry shook

Albert by the hand.

'Keep in touch. I know you won't get much sleep but ring me when you're done. Make sure your mobile is fully charged just in case anybody needs to ring you.'

'I will, Harry. Don't forget you are giving Lech a hand tomorrow. Eddie is expecting you at the pub at midday.'

'No problem,' said Harry and with that he returned to his car and drove off.

17.

Although Albert was tired, and desperate for some sleep, he knew that the next couple of hours were crucial to their planned disposal of the body parts of Trax. Besides the wrapped parcels of body parts, Albert also dragged into the living area the heavy canvas bags that he and Harry had previously stowed on the boat.

Removing the contents which had earlier been purchased by Lech, Albert saw lengths of wire and a series of barbell weights which had caused the bags to weigh as much as they did.

There were also some heavy-duty gloves, a pair of bolt cutters and a strong pair of large pliers. Although the body parts had been extensively wrapped they had started to emit a whiff of decomposition which Albert found to be quite unpleasant.

For this reason he had decided to prepare his parcels one at a time. First of all, he picked up what was obviously the head and was quite surprised again at how heavy it weighed. His first task was to secure one of the barbell weights to the packaged head using the heavy-duty wire and pliers. Once this had been done to his satisfaction, he then wrapped another layer of plastic sheeting, which had been cut to size, around the head and barbell weight and secured this with thick wire.

Albert was satisfied with his work and he proceeded to work on the remaining parcels. There were eight more on which to work and these included the four pieces of limbs and the four packages containing parts of the torso. The torso parts were a problem because of their size. They both required extra weights to be added to the package but after a couple of hours of fairly intensive work, Albert had completed the job in hand and after removing the load to the stern, he covered and secured the mound with one of the tarpaulins.

Albert retired to the kitchen area and made himself a cup of tea and jumped into a sleeping bag. Sleep didn't come easy to him as he lay thinking about what had happened and what lay in store.

Outside the boat the wind had picked up and this caused the Scarpa to rock gently. This effect helped Albert to grab some much-needed sleep.

18.

The following day was a typical mid-winter day which would make ordinary mortals huddle around a fire with a good box set to watch on the television, but Harry, Lech and especially Albert, had important work to occupy their time.

Harry and Lech arrived at the Princess Victoria and Lech drove his van into the courtyard after Eddie had opened the gates. The gates were secured behind them. All three men set about getting rid of all the evidence of their previous toils.

The cellar clearance included disposing of the shopping bags, plastic sheeting, cable ties, plastic goggles, crowbar, jemmies, torches, a plethora of discarded plastic gloves, boiler suits and other assorted materials which had been used in the abduction and murder of the beast.

These items were all loaded into the cleaning van and once this was completed, the van, with Lech driving and Harry in the passenger seat, made their way to the council recycling site.

After their departure, Eddie hosed down the cellar area once again and ensured that no trace of their criminal enterprise had been left behind.

Because of the miserable weather, the number of people disposing of household rubbish at the Council Recycling site was at an absolute minimum. The council employee was familiar with Lech and his van and, as the weather was inclement, the two men were allowed unfettered access to dispose of their rubbish without question or supervision.

Sticking to the recycling rules, the disposables were placed into the appropriate containers. Lech was pleased to see an amount of rubbish already in the containers but saw that there was still enough room for more rubbish to be laid on top. The two men completed their task and as they left they waved cheerily to the council worker sheltering in his hut by the exit gate. He was sitting next to a heater reading his tabloid newspaper. He returned their wave and moved closer to the electric heater in his cabin.

Lech dropped off Harry at his house and then went to his favoured car wash which was open every hour of the day. He paid extra above the going rate for the van to be thoroughly steam cleaned, inside and out.

19.

That same morning, aboard the narrow boat, Albert was awoken by dogs barking in the distance. He pulled back the net curtain and surveyed the scene.

The towpath would normally have been used by dog walkers and their charges. They were few in number this morning. Cyclists furiously pedalled to workplaces. The more leisurely cyclists used the path for fitness or for pleasure but because of the incessant rain the only signs of life were narrow boats moored alongside the towpath emitting thin trails of smoke from their thin chimneys indicating that some of the canal boats were occupied. In fact, Albert caught a whiff of bacon and eggs and this made him wish he had brought aboard some provisions. He had to content himself with a cup of tea. The previous occupiers had been kind enough to leave some tea bags but unfortunately there was no milk. No matter, he had a job in hand and didn't want to be distracted.

He first checked that his wrapped parcels were still as he had left them and went to start up the boat's engine. He allowed it to remain idling in neutral gear. Albert released the two securing ropes, jumped back aboard and selected the forward gear, carefully manoeuvring away from the bank of the towpath. Presumably because of the rain there was no traffic on the canal, so Albert was able to steer down the middle of the waterway.

A lone jogger, soaked and miserable looking, trudged in the other direction. Apart from the runner Albert didn't see anyone else. One of the stationary barges he passed displayed a flickering television screen.

Albert journeyed towards Limehouse where he had researched that part of the canal. He knew that two hundred yards short of the lock, the water was deeper than usual. Albert had also researched the various depths of the rest of the waterway. On one of his walks he had asked one of the boat residents how deep the canal was. The boat owner had told him that in some places the canal was quite shallow but in other places it was over eight feet deep. The old man had told Albert that he wouldn't want to fall in as the water was filthy.

Albert chose a spot that wasn't overlooked by tower blocks or flats and that was well clear of other boats.

Albert carefully steered the boat towards the right-hand side of the canal where some overhanging branches from a large willow tree draped itself over the canal like a skirt, causing the water to appear stagnant. He engaged neutral gear and the boat slowly came to a halt, almost as if treading water.

Albert picked up the wrapped head of Trax which had been weighted and secured. He made sure that he was unobserved as he slipped the package into the freezing water just like a fisherman would release a captured salmon or carp back into its natural habitat. With the one exception, of course, in that this capture did not swim gratefully away. This one dropped like a stone to the bottom of the canal where Albert hoped it would remain for ever more.

Using his map which had been provided by the boat rental company, Albert steered slowly onwards towards Limehouse, where he repeated the same manoeuvre. He placed a section of the torso of the beast in the water, once again ensuring that he wasn't being overlooked by either residents ashore or by residents afloat. The torso was very heavy and awkward and Albert was relieved that the footpath was deserted because of the prevailing weather conditions. There were no buildings overlooking the dispatch of Trax's body part. Albert slipped it into the dirty water with barely a splash.

Albert engaged gear and moved to a wider part of the navigation canal which enabled him to turn the boat around. He steered in a northerly direction passing the great big bowl of the sports stadium where his football team attempted to play something resembling football.

The disposal process of the body parts was repeated along the canal, the burial sites being carefully selected away from prying eyes. Albert ensured as much as possible that he wasn't being overlooked in the process of this distribution.

The stopping and starting was time-consuming but after about three hours Albert had completed his task depositing the various parcels at intervals stretching from Limehouse, through Hackney Wick, up to Clapton and onwards towards the lower reaches of Hertfordshire.

Albert moored up in a vacant spot and rang Harry's mobile.

'Job done, where are you?' asked Albert.

'Lech and I have finished our disposal at the Council recycling centre and I'm back indoors. What's next?' asked Harry.

'I need to clean the boat, but I'm also very hungry. I could eat a scabby horse, so I'm going to moor up near Leabridge Road and pop up and have a pint and some grub in the Ship pub.'

Albert then set about washing down all decks and surfaces with a hose, mop, bucket and cleaning cloths. He was satisfied with his work.

He started up the engine again, released the ropes and made his way to Leyton. Spotting a gap in the parked traffic of canal boats of all shapes, sizes and colours, he secured himself to the towpath and locked the living compartment.

Albert sprinted up the stone steps and into the welcoming warmth of the Ship where he ordered a fry-up of gargantuan proportions.

He was only just into his foaming pint of IPA when, through the door, emerged the figures of Lech and Harry.

After hugs and handshakes all round, Lech and Harry also ordered food similar to that which Albert had ordered. More drinks were bought. Albert described his work from the previous evening and his morning's work.

'I've marked where I've dropped him off with a series of buoys with a little red flag,' said Albert.

Albert saw a worried look on Lech's face,

'Only kidding. I don't want to be too presumptuous, but everything seems to have gone perfectly. Provided we're careful, we might even get away with this. No matter what happens now, something had to be done.'

Albert was pleased to see that the other two compatriots were as enthusiastic about their prospects as he was. The meal was enjoyed with great gusto and Lech said with a serious voice, 'Be careful what you tell Eddie.'

'What do you mean?' a concerned Harry asked.

'He will go mad if you tell him this food is better than his.'

All three laughed out loud. The diminutive publican behind the bar could not understand why three grown men were so happy on such a miserable day in the middle of winter.

After the meal, Albert returned to the boat and steered towards the boat's official mooring. Darkness had descended and he ensured that the boat was secure in every aspect. He faced a long walk in the cold across the Marshes but in the distance he spotted one solitary car parked with its lights off next to the changing rooms which were used during the respective seasons of football, rugby and cricket. Albert could see now that it was Lech's cleaning van and, with all three men huddled in the front compartment, they set off for home.

As they were about to near the park Albert said, 'Drop me here, Lech, I want to have a walk through the park. With that big fucking lump gone it should be a lot safer for people to make use of the park.'

'It will be a walk in the park,' smiled Harry, 'I'll come

with you, Albert,' he continued.

Both men alighted from the vehicle and strode towards the southern entrance to the park. At first Albert thought the park was deserted but in the gloom he could just about see a group of four figures huddled below a large oak bereft of its leaves.

'Woof, woof.'

Albert couldn't believe his ears. Somebody was using the death of his old pal Buddy in an obvious effort to goad him. He spun on his heels and started to march back towards the source of the taunt.

'Leave it out, Albert, don't do anything silly' said Harry.

There was no stopping an enraged Albert. Harry followed him over to where the taunt had come from. Slouching with his hands in his tracksuit bottoms, Albert recognised the sallow features of the Pakistani he knew as Saf.

'What did you say?' Albert asked.

'You heard,' came the sneered reply.

'Where's your dog?' The Asian started laughing. Two other dark shapes in the background started to giggle.

'See this,' said Albert, producing the nose ring of Trax from his pocket.

'Recognise it?' He placed the ring two inches from Saf's face. Initially a look of puzzlement crossed Saf's face and then it suddenly dawned on him what Albert was holding and his eyes widened in disbelief.

'You're fucking next,' said Albert. 'Do I make myself clear?' There was no response from the shocked youth.

'Do I make myself fucking clear?' Albert shouted into his face. Saf was too dumbstruck to reply.

Harry pulled Albert away and out of earshot of the gang he said, 'What the fuck did you do that for. You're admitting that we have got rid of him. You need to get rid of that ring straight away. I can't believe you just did that. That is a serious mistake, Albert. What the fuck have you done? Get rid of that thing now. They will come back at you. They won't let this go.'

'I'm sorry, Harry, I lost it,' Albert replied.

They walked home in silence. Albert reflected that he had made a mistake and had let his feelings get the better of him. This had been the first hiccup since this plan had first been muted and executed, but it was a major blip as it gave away their innocence, albeit to a group they didn't recognise as a threat to their freedom.

Just before they reached their respective houses, Albert pulled the ring from his pocket and slipped it down a street drain.

'I'm sorry, Harry, I shouldn't have done that.'

Harry didn't reply but went indoors with barely a look at Albert.

20.

Southgate Police Station housed the temporary offices of
the Area Murder Investigation team. All over London
some of the Met's finest detectives were split into regional
squads with the specific task of dealing with serious crime
and in particular, murder.

William Cronk had dealt with his fair share of murders
over the last few years and had become somewhat non-
plussed about young blacks killing each other but this
latest case was different. He had actually met the family of
young Marcia, the McDonalds employee, and his usually
tough-as-teak outward appearance melted a little when he
met her mother and her sibling brothers. Cronk was quite
shaken by the flow of tears. He was impressed by the clean-
liness of the house despite the lack of finances.

Cronk sat in his office contemplating the case. His office
was compact and although there was no street window he
was able to look out into the main murder squad office. A
row of desks running down the left-hand wall were occupied by computers at which sat a variety of personnel,
mainly women, who clacked away at their respective key-
boards inputting data and cross-referencing statements and

reports.

Interspersed between the computers was a battery of telephones and even from within his goldfish bowl of an office, Cronk could hear the chatter and the cacophony of keys being pounded ceaselessly.

William Cronk, or, Old Bill, as his troops had nicknamed him, was a huge man, six foot five inches tall and built like a second row forward, which he had been some years ago. But now, age was catching up with him and retirement from the Service beckoned.

His health was not as good as it could have been. He had often reflected on his career and how he had been overlooked for further promotion once he had reached the rank of Detective Chief Inspector. He now conceded privately that the new young breed of university graduates were going to reach and overtake him on the promotion ladder. It didn't matter to the powers that be, that these upstarts couldn't detect their own way home after a couple of pints and lacked common sense in everything they did.

He was also proud of the fact that he had an unblemished record when it came to solving murders.

Having thought about it, though, William Cronk was quite happy about his present situation. Apart from his health, that is. He had at his disposal a squad of personally handpicked detectives who were industrious. They worked hard which was all he ever asked for.

Cronk's stature was enhanced by a huge bald head featuring a couple of old rugby scars. He ran a tight ship with no excessive drinking, although a five o' clock office meeting led on occasions to a bottle of whisky being produced. This little treat had a dual purpose as it rewarded those who had put in a day's shift but also encouraged most of the others to say their piece and speak their minds.

One such office meeting was scheduled for later that afternoon after the civilian typists had locked up their computers for the day and gone home.

Cronk had as his assistant a young Detective Sergeant called Elaine Webster. Her unofficial title was that of bag carrier, but her position was important insomuch as she was responsible for providing the glue that kept Cronk's show on the road. She was an important liaison between the civilian in-putters and the detectives. She was at Cronk's beck and call and she made sure that he was kept up to date with everything that was happening as well as providing copious amounts of coffee to sustain Old Bill.

Cronk very rarely left the goldfish bowl. He would bring in a tupperware box of freshly made sandwiches and when they had been devoured, and hunger had got the better of him, a young detective constable would be dispatched to the pastry shop three doors away to provide for the sustenance of Detective Chief Inspector Cronk.

At five pm the squad members filed into the larger office. Cronk had a quick look around and all of the regular members were present, either standing around the edge of the room or sitting on the chairs vacated by the civilian typists. Cronk also noticed two faces he didn't recognise.

'Welcome to the meeting. I'm going to hand it over to DS Webster who will summarise where we are at with this enquiry,' said Cronk.

'Before we start,' said Webster, 'I want to introduce DC's

Davis and Cambell from the Criminal Intelligence Department at New Scotland Yard.' She pointed towards the two new faces in the room, both of whom nodded. Webster continued, 'As you are all aware, a double murder occurred at McDonalds in Tottenham High Road two weeks ago. The first victim was shot at point blank range by a masked and helmeted youth who had an accomplice dressed in similar attire. This first victim was identified as Joshua Mills and it has been established that he was a member of a Tottenham gang called Black Lightning. This gang consists mainly of black youths and their criminal enterprises include robbery, drug dealing and running the odd protection racket. Just a fairly normal gang in this present day and age. One of hundreds in London. The two other gang members that Mills was with, have not been identified as yet, and are being sought as a matter of urgency with a view to them being witnesses.'

'Some hope,' somebody muttered from the back of the room before Webster continued, 'The other victim was a young black girl called Marcia Williams. She was an employee at McDonalds and bravely, if not foolishly, attempted to block the exit of the gunman. She was shot through her left eye socket and died immediately. I should add that Mills was shot in the neck, the bullet entering downwards into his lungs and he was dead within five minutes. Bullets and casings were retrieved and submitted to the Firearms section at the Metropolitan Police Forensic Laboratory but with no good results so far. Fingerprinting the scene reveals that the assailants were wearing gloves, as were the two gang members who avoided being shot. A

Kawasaki 250 cc motorbike was used as the murderer's getaway but this has been found abandoned near Bruce Grove. It was burnt out with no useful leads coming from this angle. Needless to say there are no witnesses to this crime. It's typical, I'm afraid, of the area and considering the violence used it's understandable why ordinary people don't want to get involved.'

'I'm going to go around the room asking you all to update the guv'nor and me of what you have been up to in the last couple of days. After this meeting has finished and before we have a beer, I want you to upload your reports onto the computers.'

Ds Webster then introduced DC's Davis and Cambell. DC Alan Davis did all the talking.

'Good evening, as you are all aware my colleague and I are based at New Scotland Yard at Criminal Intelligence. Part of our particular remit is to identify and track the movements of criminal gangs, and in particular, those of the new breed of black London gangs. The deceased male, Joshua Mills, as you know now, was a member of a gang based in Tottenham. This gang is known by members as Black Lightning as your Detective Sergeant rightly identified. These gangs are mostly territorial and stick to their own patch where they terrorise the local communities and will use varying degrees of violence to further their own ends. However, Black Lightning recently have not restricted themselves to their own area and our enquiries, assisted by surveillance and the robust use of our extensive informants operation, has revealed that this group are not shy when it comes to trespassing onto areas outside their own patch.'

'We are currently looking at information that shows that members of this gang have been making themselves busy in east and south London. It is possible that this murder may be a message to this gang to cease their operations in areas not under their control.'

Cronk had been listening attentively and asked the detective

'How close are you to pinpointing other areas of London that this gang has encroached onto?'

'We are currently utilising CCTV footage and other sources but as you can understand this takes a lifetime of work and I am hopeful that by using our own covert surveillance and use of registered informants we may be able to answer that question more effectively in the next few days. However, I can say that movement has been spotted and identified in the Plaistow and Stratford areas of east London. As well as Peckham in south London.'

The two Scotland yard officers then updated the murder squad, as best they could, on the identities of the other gang members of Black Lightning.

A pack of light beers and canned lager were produced and a more relaxed atmosphere pervaded the squad room. Cronk sat on the edge of a desk with a plastic cup of foul-tasting coffee from the vending machine down the corridor. His bag carrier, DS Elaine Webster, had no such inhibitions and sipped from a bottle of beer.

'Who do we know from Plaistow or Forest Gate that might be able to help us? Whose brains can we pick, Elaine?' asked Cronk.

'When I worked at Stoke Newington I worked with a young Detective Constable called John McEvoy. Do you want me to speak to him?'

'No, I think we'll do this officially. Find out for me what station he's working at and get me the name of his Detective Inspector.'

Webster disappeared into the goldfish bowl and raised the phone number of Forest Gate police station from Cronk's computer. The details flashed up that McEvoy did indeed work out of that station and his Detective Inspector was a certain Detective Inspector David Marker. Webster waved at Cronk and he came back into his own office.

'McEvoy is stationed at Forest Gate and his DI is a man called David Marker,' Webster informed her boss.

'I know Marker,' said Cronk, 'I'll give him a ring in the morning.'

The next morning after Cronk had sorted himself out after reading the overnight reports and grabbing himself a polystyrene cup of coffee from the machine, he settled into his chair and picked up the phone and rang the Detective Inspector at Forest Gate Police station.

'Good morning, is that Dave Marker?'

'It is,' said the voice on the other end of the phone, 'Who is this?'

'You know me from a few years ago, but then, you never were much of a detective. It doesn't seem you have improved any over the years.'

'You old bastard Cronk, are you still alive?' said Marker, laughing. 'You're obviously not playing rugby anymore.

You must be in your seventies,' still laughing. 'What can I do for you?'

'I would like to borrow one of your DC's. A DC McEvoy. Just to help us out with a problem at this end which might benefit us both. It's in relation to a murder we are investigating. Our murderers may have a link to your patch and young McEvoy has his ear to the ground, I hear, and he might be able to help us.'

'I'll fix it up,' replied Marker.

Later that morning Detective Inspector Marker looked out from his office and called Detective Constable McEvoy into his office.

'Come in, John, and close the door behind you. A Detective Chief Inspector Cronk is leading a murder enquiry out of Southgate Police station. They are investigating the murder of that young black girl who got caught in the crossfire in that shooting at McDonalds in Tottenham. Do you know the one I'm talking about?'

'Yes, guvnor, she was an innocent bystander just doing her job from what I read. She obviously wasn't the target. It's been all over the papers and London television news.'

'Yes, that's the one. Anyway, Cronk thinks you can be of some assistance to his squad and wants to borrow you for a few days. Will you be able to cope with that and still manage your workload at this end?' asked Marker.

'No problem, sir, I can always pop in from time to time to keep on top of what's on my desk.'

'Make sure you do, John, because it's quite important that we know what they know about our own patch. If

Southgate has got any info about our manor it's vital that I know all about it. Do I make myself clear? We need to be in control of what is happening here, understand?'

'Absolutely, guvnor, I'll debrief you regularly,' replied McEvoy.

21.

John McEvoy tidied up his desk at Forest Gate Police Station and logged out of his computer after writing up a couple of reports. He drove to Southgate Police Station where he presented himself to Detective Chief Inspector Cronk. Cronk was sitting with a coffee behind his desk in the goldfish bowl. He waved to McEvoy to sit down and said to the young detective, 'Avoid that coffee machine down the corridor. You'll finish up in the morgue drinking that stuff. Now, as you probably are aware, I am leading a team of detectives into a double murder. The intended victim was a young black gang member. I am not going to lose any sleep about his death although I will obviously go through the appropriate motions. What I'm more concerned with is the fact that an innocent young girl was caught up in the crossfire and her death is nothing short of a tragedy for her, her family and her friends. We have had information from Criminal Intelligence that the perpetrators were seeking to send a message to the Tottenham Black Lightning gang that they should stick to their own territory and not trespass onto other areas of London.'

'We also suspect that the Tottenham gang have been

making themselves busy in your area of London, namely Forest Gate and its surrounds. If we assume that to be the case it means that the murderer comes from your patch and I can tell you now that before I hand in my resignation papers, nothing would fill me more with pride than to convict the animal who has done this.'

'I understand that, Sir. I will do whatever I can to help.' replied McEvoy

'DS Webster, my bag carrier, will make sure you are authorised to research our computers. This will enable you to access all statements and evidence that we are in possession of. Hopefully this will help you to possibly identify the suspect, or suspects, at your end. I don't expect things to happen overnight but I would be grateful if you could attend this office at least once a day and in particular at five pm when we tend to have our office meetings. There should be a frank and free exchange of information. Oh, and to hopefully convince you, we usually have a beer!'

22.

ack in Stratford, life continued, but not quite as before. Albert, who had embarrassed himself with Harry, did not attend the Monday night football at the Working Men's club. The previous day, instead of having three or four pints at the Princess Victoria, Albert just had one. There was no show from Lech, and Eddie was busy behind the bar. When Mark arrived, Albert didn't fancy a lengthy conversation with him, and after one pint excused himself and walked home.

Having not been out in the taxi for a while, Albert was determined that he was going to throw himself into work and promised himself that he was going to put in a full week's shift in the cab.

During the ensuing week Albert was busy. The taxi trade usually picked up at the onset of Spring, but Albert's sleep patterns were not very good and he fretted about the discovery of body parts and the apparent breakdown of his relationships with his three accomplices. He also felt a bit embarrassed about his slip-up in front of Harry.

Albert decided that he needed a break from his usual lifestyle so on returning the cab to Ray at the end of the week he said to him,

'Does your brother still have that place in Spain?'

'He does, and he's back in the UK at the moment. If you wanted to rent it at a basement price, now is the time, as he would want someone to keep it ticking over whilst he's not there. You've been there before. And the weather is gradually getting better.'

On Sunday, after a full week's work, Albert went to the Princess Victoria. Eddie was behind the bar.

'Eddie, I'm off to Ray's brother's place in Spain. I fancy a bit of sunshine and I'm not sleeping well. I think the break will do me a bit of good.'

'Ok, Albert, chill out and relax. The fact that nothing seems to have happened is in our favour. The longer it goes on like this the better.'

'Eddie, will you tell Lech when he comes in, please?'

Albert did not stop for a pint and when he left he bumped into Mark on his way in.

'Not stopping Albert?'

'No, Mark, I'm going away for a few days of better weather. This miserable stuff is depressing me.'

Mark nodded his goodbyes and entered the public house.

Upon reaching his home address Albert knocked on his next-door neighbour's door. The big frame of Harry appeared.

'Harry, I'm off to Spain for a few days. Just to let you know the house will be empty.'

'Ok, Albert, thanks for letting me know. Hope you

come back refreshed, and in control of your actions.'

Albert accepted this as a form of admonishment. Something he couldn't argue with. He knew he had made a mistake, a misjudgement, but hoped it wouldn't affect what had been an operation carried out with military-like precision.

23.

After he had secured a flight on the internet from Stansted to Alicante, Albert Oxford packed enough items of clothing for a few days' break on the Costa Blanca.

The two-hour flight passed by, uninterrupted by turbulence, and on landing the first thing that hit Albert was the notable increase in temperature.

Albert forked out thirty-five euros for a taxi to take him to the apartment which would be his base for his break from the hell that was East London.

On arrival at the apartment Albert entered through the gate to the complex and in a wall mounted security key box he punched in the numbers which would release the keys to the apartment.

Inside the apartment he read the housekeeping notes left by Ray's brother, Charlie, and had a quick stock take. In the fridge were bottles of fresh water and a pack of San Miguel beers. The temperature throughout the day did not require the air conditioning to be switched on and the television was a wide screen wall-mounted set with controls giving access to all English channels and Sky Sports.

A small kitchen allowed him to have meals in the apartment and the bathroom facilities had been upgraded and consisted of a walk-in shower. Albert made a list of supplies that he would need from the supermarket two blocks away. Albert punched in the wifi code into his mobile phone and then left the flat to buy his groceries.

The temperature was a comfortable ten degrees above what he had left in the UK and he only needed a light jacket. Once the shopping had been completed Albert returned to the flat and stowed away his purchases. The Spanish town was situated about 30 miles north of Alicante and sat very near the coast. Albert knew the area from a previous visit but he needed to take the travel cramp out of his legs and took a short stroll along the seafront a couple of blocks from his apartment. It already felt like a different world and Albert Oxford was slowly, but surely, beginning to put the dark memories to the back of his mind.

Over the course of the next few days Albert's routine developed into a fairly regular habit. Getting up fairly early, he would have his morning cup of tea on the small balcony, catching the early morning sunshine before it disappeared to his right. The television would be switched on and was just loud enough for him to hear the latest UK and world news from his position on the balcony.

After digesting the latest news from home and abroad, he would have a light breakfast of cereal and toast.

Mid-morning saw Albert take a walk into town and a fairly energetic walk along the seafront before stopping at his favourite cafe for brunch. After his meal he walked back through the town shopping-front and this enabled him to purchase an English newspaper.

Back at the apartment he would scour every page to update himself on the latest happenings in the outside world. He allowed himself a more than cursory glance at the sports pages keeping himself abreast of the goings-on of his football team. More often than not this would be followed by a little afternoon snooze.

After awakening, a choice had to be made of either cooking for himself or using one of the cheap restaurants in the busy little town. After his evening repaste he made himself comfortable in the flat and indulged in a bit of British television, and if lucky, a game of football on Sky Sports. A solid sleep followed, undisturbed by barking dogs, police sirens and fireworks.

Albert thought to himself that he could stay here forever but knew that his break was destined to finish sometime in the near future.

24.

During Albert Oxford's absence, the double murder investigation conducted out of Southgate Police station was proceeding at a leisurely pace. McEvoy busied himself looking at various reports and the few witness statements that had been taken.

The witness statements were minimalist as he expected and did not shed any light on possible suspects. Of interest to McEvoy were the reports from the two Criminal Intelligence detectives who relied on informants and other intelligence-based technology involving the usage of known mobile phone data.

Of particular interest to John McEvoy was the fact that the Intelligence officers seemed to be focusing their attention on the gang led by Trax. McEvoy knew that the Intelligence officers would be at the office meeting the following day so he was determined to speak to the two officers privately.

The following day the office meeting was conducted by DCI William Cronk and after the junior officers had made their input, the atmosphere in the squad room became more relaxed with the introduction of a couple of packs of beers. McEvoy grabbed a bottle of Carlsberg and approached the two Scotland Yard men.

'From reading through the reports, it seems that you are swayed to the idea that the gang involved is the Stratford gang that mainly operate on my patch under the control of Forest Gate Police.'

'Yes, that's right. And as you are no doubt aware the so-called leader of that gang is a big lump of a West Indian called Trax. He is a nasty bastard as you probably know. We know from phone monitoring that his cell phone has been inactive for a few days now.' The taller of the two detectives, Campbell, added,

'It has also come to our attention that he seems to have disappeared off the face of the earth.'

'That fits everything,' replied McEvoy, 'that area has gone very quiet, which is quite a pleasant change for us.'

'What do you know about Trax?' Campbell asked John McEvoy.

'He's a vicious thug, a nasty bully, and he has made the local peoples' lives unbearable. He leads a gang who specialise in drug dealing, robbery, extortion, assault and battery. Unfortunately, he is running wild and that is because we cannot get one single soul to stand up and give evidence against him. If he has disappeared, could it be that someone from this Tottenham gang has had him whacked?'

'Unlikely.' replied Campbell, 'The Tottenham crew are aware that we are looking at them. It could be that Trax has upset somebody from his neck of the woods. From what we hear, he upset a lot of people when he hung a dog from a tree as well as all the usual shit he gets up to.'

'I can't understand why he would hang a dog from a tree?' said McEvoy

'Apparently it was done to wind up, and annoy one of the locals he had had a run in with,' replied DC Davis. 'We picked up a conversation on his own personal mobile, not one of the burners that he uses all the time.'

McEvoy remained silent and thought to himself as he sipped from his bottle of lager. The one local he knew who had got under the skin of Trax was Albert Oxford. He decided that he should pay Albert Oxford a visit to see what he knew, if anything.

The following morning John McEvoy went to Forest Gate Police Station to pick up any correspondence he may have received and to check on the progress of case papers from a separate case that he had submitted to the Crown Prosecution Service. While he was sitting at his desk he was aware that his Detective Inspector, David Marker, was hovering in the doorway.

'It's about time, John, for you to update me on how the investigation is going. Pop into my office when you've finished with your correspondence and you can fill me in.'

Ten minutes later John McEvoy was sitting in front of Marker's desk.

'Tell all, John, please' asked Marker. McEvoy then proceeded to tell his boss how the investigation was progressing and also the thoughts of the two detectives from Criminal Intelligence. After he had finished the Detective

Inspector said, 'Is that it?'

'Not quite,' McEvoy replied, 'they mentioned something about a dog being hung by its neck in the park.'

'What's that got to do with anything?' asked Marker.

'Well,' said McEvoy, 'Scotland Yard's finest brains think it was to do with getting back at one of the locals.'

Marker rested his chin on his hands and mused, 'Do they really? How interesting. And you're telling me that this piece of shit, Trax, has disappeared? Well, what I think, John, for what it's worth is, fucking good riddance!'

McEvoy smiled at this surprising outburst from his boss and said, 'Is that all, guvnor? I'll need to get back to Southgate.'

'Yes that's ok John,' replied Marker. 'and make sure you keep me updated.'

The following Sunday Lech strode into the saloon bar of The Princess Victoria and sat at the bar where he grabbed the attention of Eddie, 'You okay, Eddie. No news is good news. Is that what you English say?'

'Yes indeed, Lech,' replied the rotund landlord, 'and people seem to be in a better mood since our friend went on his holidays.'

'Ha!' laughed Lech, 'do you mean our friend who has gone to Spain, or the one who has gone scuba diving?'

'Probably a bit of both.' said Eddie, adding, 'Our friend from Espanol probably needed a break, whereas our diving champion definitely needed a longer break. I should think both of them are fairly relaxed at the moment.'

Both men smiled and at that moment the regular

Sunday lunchtime customer, Mark, walked in and joined them at the bar.

'Where's Albert?' asked Mark, 'I thought he would have been here, especially today, as his team won yesterday. I thought I was going to get bored by him telling me how good they were.'

'He is just having a little break,' said Eddie, 'a few days away with a bit of warming sunshine. He has been grafting hard in the taxi for a while.'

'Anywhere nice?' asked Mark, 'Lucky bugger, at this time of the year, what with this weather we're having.'

'The guy he rents the cab from, Ray. His brother, Charlie has got a place in Spain and he is renting it for a few days,' replied Eddie.

'As I said, lucky sod at this time of the year,' said Mark. 'Wish it was me.'

After his obligatory two pints, Mark left on his own, leaving Lech to demolish a fair proportion of the roast potatoes served up by Eddie's kitchen staff.

25.

The he following day McEvoy travelled to Southgate Police station and when he arrived he was summoned into the office of DCI Cronk who had with him Detective Sergeant Webster.

'John, as you know our friends from the Yard are thinking along the lines that this Trax monster has disappeared and that it has more to do with your part of London rather than the Tottenham end. I want you to focus on anybody, or anything, which might lead us to the whereabouts of Trax because at the moment, and without a lot to go on, he seems to be our best bet at the moment.'

..

The following morning McEvoy rang Albert Oxford's mobile phone and was somewhat surprised that the long ringtone signified that the recipient was abroad in a foreign country.

When Albert's phone rang he was sitting on the wall of the marina watching the tourist sail boats fill up with holiday makers eager to sail round the local caves.

'Is that you, Mr Oxford?' asked McEvoy. 'What are you doing abroad and where are you?'

'Just having a few days break,' answered Albert, 'what can I help you with?'

'Nothing important. It's about our friend Trax. I need to ask you a few questions. When are you back in the UK?' asked McEvoy.

Albert told him he would be back at the end of the week and made an appointment to see McEvoy the following Monday at Forest Gate Police Station. Albert thought about McEvoy's invitation to see him. He thought to himself that if it had been important McEvoy wouldn't have been so casual about it.

26.

Harry left by his street door shouting out to his wife Libby that he was off to Smithfield for his weekly trip to the Smithfield Meat Market to see his mates and to have a pint, or three, in the Cock Tavern. He closed his garden gate and turned towards the direction of the underground station which would take him on the Central Line to St Paul's tube station. After only a few yards he was aware of two figures both sitting astride motorbikes. Both were wearing crash helmets and were dressed in dark hoodies, denim jeans and trainers.

He could see that they were paying him close attention but made no move to follow him and they remained motionless on their respective machines.

Harry had a bit of lunch with his mates and a few pints, and after saying his farewells he made the journey home with his little parcel of free meat, a gift from his pal, Archie.

As he approached his address Harry saw that the motorbikes had gone but sitting on the wall opposite his house were the same two hoodies, this time without crash helmets. They were sitting on the wall of the house belonging to Mo Connors.

Harry placed his parcel of meat inside his front porch and went across the road. Although their hoods were up, there was no mistaking the long angular nose of the Pakistani called Saf.

'What are you two doing here?' asked Harry

'Bruv, it's none of your business, we can go where we like, innit?' replied Saf.

'The old lady who lives here doesn't like people sitting on her wall. It makes the place look untidy. If you don't fucking clear off, I'll chop your fucking heads off. Do I make myself clear?'

Both youths moved away sullenly muttering under their breath.

27.

The following morning Harry looked out of his bedroom window through the net curtain and saw that the two youths on their motorbikes had resumed their vigil. When Harry walked across to the paper shop, both drove off.

Later that afternoon Harry heard next door's garden gate swing open and through his front room window saw Albert with a small suitcase walking up the path to his front door. Before Albert could enter Harry appeared and said to him, 'Albert, just to warn you that a couple of those rats from the park have been hanging around here. I'm fairly sure they're not interested in me, cos I had a go at them yesterday. Which leads me to the conclusion that it's you they're looking for. One of them is the prick with the long nose and a weedy little Asian bastard with yellow teeth. I would be careful if I were you.'

'Thanks Harry, it's nice to be popular. That detective wants to see me on Monday morning. Something to do with Trax. Can't be urgent or I would have had my collar felt when I landed at Stansted.'

'The talk down at the club is that Trax has gone on his holidays,' said Harry. 'Everybody living round here seems to know he's not about at the moment and it's lifted the whole area. It has given everyone a bit of a boost.'

'Wonder where he's gone on holiday?' smiled Albert.

'Nowhere exotic,' replied Harry, 'probably stayed local. Be careful, Albert.'

Albert was pleased that Harry had appeared to have forgiven him for his recent lapse.

After Albert had unpacked his suitcase he prepared himself one of his microwave meals taken from the freezer. A glass of red wine and then the prospect of a walk to the stadium to watch his team attempt to lift themselves out of the relegation zone.

Friday night football was a novelty and only occurred in order to satisfy the demands of Sky television and although he could have watched the game on television there was no substitute for the atmosphere generated at a crunch match, even at this relatively early stage of a fight to avoid relegation from the upper tier of football.

Although it was a Friday evening, Eddie felt confident enough to leave his two barmaids in charge of the clientele in The Princess Victoria. The pub wouldn't be too busy as a few of the regulars had gone to watch the game and those that were in the bar watching the game on the box were doing their level best to stretch half a pint of beer over two hours. *Bloody cheapskates*, thought Eddie, but at least he knew the bar wasn't going to be busy for the next couple of hours. When the game finished it would definitely get busier.

Eddie walked the two hundred yards to where the lock-up garages were situated in a street opposite the cemetery. Opening his garage door Eddie climbed into his big comfortable beast of a dark green Volvo estate. He settled into the leather upholstery, switched on a bit of music and drove out of the lock-up garage area.

Eddie's task tonight was to go down to the local Cash and Carry to stock up on trays of soft drinks and mixers. He would add to the shopping list a number of bottles of spirits. These extras would be in addition to what the brewery supplied him with, and by careful substitution here and there, he would be able to skim off a healthy profit which would go towards his retirement fund.

..

Albert Oxford set off for the twenty-five-minute walk to the stadium. He was not aware of being followed by anybody. As he neared the stadium the crowds of supporters began to thicken and after queuing to get past security, Albert ascended the steps into the big bowl of the stadium which had been host to the 2012 London Olympics.

On seeing the bright green grass lit up by the powerful floodlights he still got excited at the sight and prospect of top-class football played under floodlights and played out virtually on his doorstep.

The deliberately timed five minutes he had allowed himself before kick-off, gave Albert the opportunity to greet his regular season ticket holder neighbours and to quickly discuss the team selected by the under-pressure team coach.

The game itself was not of a high standard but was made more exciting by the nervousness of the situation, with both teams desperate to win, in an attempt to ease their respective relegation fears.

At half time Albert availed himself of a watery pint of lager in a plastic glass and returned to his seat to see his team take a two-goal lead. They hung on nervously for an important win which was only just about deserved on the balance of play.

As the referee blew for full time, there was a mass exodus of sixty thousand people from the arena. Albert had to endure the tight crush of fans but it was made easier by the excited hubbub of chatter by the masses, relieved by the consequences of the result.

The hordes steadily shuffled slowly towards the exit checkpoints. Heaving their way towards the Underground station the steam of perspiration from the mass of supporters was highlighted by the tall arc lamps positioned strategically along the exit routes. The burger vans and other fast-food franchises were doing a roaring trade buoyed obviously by the result.

Once the Underground station had been reached the crowd thinned dramatically, as the large majority of the home support were dispersed to all parts of London and Essex, whilst others took advantage of the numerous food outlets in the huge shopping centre that was Westfield.

The huge crowd had now dissipated and no longer existed. Albert found that the further he got away from the stadium, and the nearer he got to his home, he was aware that he was quite alone, save for the odd straggler like himself making their way home. He looked over his shoulder every few moments but saw nobody.

Because of the warning from Harry earlier in the day, Albert decided that he would not go near the park but planned on taking a longer route home in an effort to frustrate any would-be followers.

He still looked round but saw nothing and laughed at himself for being so paranoid. Walking through the back streets he found himself becoming a little nervous and was cursing himself for not sticking to the main roads.

He looked round behind again and thought he just glimpsed the headlight of a motor bike with a rider and pillion passenger, but it turned away and Albert breathed a sigh of relief.

The street that Albert had found himself walking along was poorly lit and absolutely deserted. In front of him Albert saw the motorbike and realised that it had circled the block enabling the rider to approach Albert from the front and block his passage home.

Albert looked behind him and saw a hooded figure approaching him from the other direction. Both routes of escape were now cut off, forcing Albert to make a decision. He could take on the one on foot, but the motorbike would be quickly onto him. The other thing which disturbed Albert was that he could see in the distance a glimpse of shiny metal in the hoodie's right hand. Now it was definitely time to panic.

Both the bike rider and the hoodie were approaching him slowly from different directions. Albert feared the worst.

At that very moment, swinging into view, Albert saw a big green Volvo. It pulled up beside him and a beaming Eddie said, 'SAS to the rescue, Albert. Private Eddie Baines at your service. Jump in quickly or would you rather walk home?

'What are you doing here, Eddie?'

'Later, Albert. What's afoot?'

'The one on foot has a knife and the knobhead on the bike is ferrying him about. Harry says they've been looking for me for a few days.'

'Time for my tank training to kick in,' smiled Eddie, 'buckle up and enjoy the ride.'

With that, Eddie engaged the gears and moved forward towards the motorbike. When he accelerated, the bike rider realised what was happening and immediately turned the bike round to flee. Eddie picked up speed and chased the rider into what appeared to be a cul-de-sac.

The tarmac glistened after the fall of the recent drizzle and Eddie propelled the car forward with engine noise increasing. The bike rider, realising that he was in a no through road and being confronted by a big car and two males, decided to take his chance and he turned around once again and came at the Volvo with the intention of veering at the last second and slipping past the offside of the saloon car.

Eddie, however, had anticipated this and deliberately left a gap big enough for the bike to get through. The bike now was whining with the noise of acceleration and as he went to draw alongside the Volvo, Eddie flicked the steering wheel and the car turned into the rider's path and hit the motorbike with a glancing blow.

The bike cartwheeled at speed and careered along the wet surface sending up a shower of sparks. As it was sliding at considerable speed, the driver and bike became detached. The rider slid on his own at great speed, his momentum coming to a sudden and dramatic halt when he slammed into a lamppost. The angle of his right leg suggested that the rider would have trouble riding his bike again, a fact also confirmed by the grotesque angle of the rider's head in relation to the rest of his body. Without doubt, a fatality.

The motorbike careered into a garden hedge and lay on its side, wheels spinning, engine revving.

Eddie turned the car around and slowly drove past the body carefully avoiding the mangled parts of the deceased. As they exited the street Albert craned his neck to see if there was any sign of the other hooded youth, but the street was deathly quiet. A sole curtain twitched and swiftly closed.

'Job done,' smiled Eddie, 'good job I had to pop out to do some shopping. I'll get rid of the shopping at the pub and stick the car back in the garage, never to see the light of day until I've made sure there's no incriminating evidence on this old beauty. Anyway, what was the score?'

Albert looked at Eddie, shaking his head.

'We won two nil.'

'Great news,' said Eddie, 'there'll be a load of happy punters in the pub. Some of them might even buy a drink!'

28.

East London Gazette

Police are appealing for witnesses after the body of a youth was found in Hamner Close. A police spokesman told the Gazette that it appeared that the unnamed youth had been the victim of a hit and run accident…

The morning after the football match, Lech was having his van cleaned at the local carwash. He knew the Romanian car-washers to speak to, and during the conversation he had with the man in charge, he was told that a motorcyclist had been killed in a street not too far away from where Lech lived. Lech asked how it had happened and he was told that it looked like the rider had been travelling at speed and had slipped on the greasy road surface crashing into a lampost. He had been killed on impact.

'Was he a local?' asked Lech.

'Yeh, one of the naughty gang that is no good,' replied the Romanian

Lech nodded and said 'Good riddance to the scumbag. Which one was it?'

'Dunno, Asian. Broke his neck,' replied the big Romanian.

After his van had been washed and dried, Lech drove to the scene of the motorbike crash. Parking his van, Lech got out and walked up the street towards a lamp post, at the bottom of which lay a number of floral tributes. Lech took a look at some of the attached cards which contained messages such as *Legend*, *Majid, luv u bruv*, and *Majid, you are a hero, you will be avenged.*

As Lech was returning to his van he spotted an elderly couple coming out of their front door and walking in his direction.

'Do you know what happened here?' asked Lech.

The old man replied, 'No, and I'd be very surprised if anybody saw anything. Everybody around here lives in fear of those idiots. At night it's like being a prisoner in your own house. This is the only time of day you feel safe to come out your front door and do some shopping.'

Grabbing her husband's arm, the woman yanked her husband away. They scuttled off in the direction of the main road, presumably to get on a bus to take them to the shopping centre.

After he had finished his days cleaning chores, Lech decided to walk round to Albert's house to tell him the news. There was no reply to his knocking but then Harry appeared at his own doorway.

Lech said to him,

'I was just looking for Albert to tell him about one of the

scumbags from the park. He crashed his bike last night and broke his neck. Nobody saw a thing.'

'Great news,' said Harry, 'I might have an extra pint tonight. We are not the only place affected, though. I've just heard on the news that another three got stabbed in Ilford last night and another one the night before in Walthamstow.'

'Maybe the locals should fight back,' said Lech, winking at Harry. Harry smiled and said,

'That's for sure. If the Old Bill or this useless Mayor of London won't do anything about it, then it would be no surprise if local people fought back.'

29.

When Sunday arrived, Albert was one of the first in the saloon bar. Friday night's experience did not seem to have had any effect on Eddie as he beamed a welcome and poured a foaming pint of ale for Albert.

'You ok, Eddie?' asked Albert

'Couldn't be better,' replied Eddie, 'I just heard another three got wasted in Ilford and another in Walthamstow. That's a hundred and fifty in the last year. Perhaps that's the plan of the London Mayor. Just to let them wipe each other out.'

'Only problem is, Eddie, when other innocent people are involved, a bit like us.'

Eddie smiled, 'I wouldn't say we were innocent, Albert, but I know what you mean. They're turning us into animals as well.'

'I've just had a lovely few day in Spain. None of this shit going on, everybody is nice to each other, nobody is scared to walk out of their front door. I would emigrate to Spain or somewhere like that at the drop of a hat.' Albert had a sip of his pint just as Lech came through the saloon bar door.

'I see another of those fuckers has gone,' said the big Pole.

'We were just talking about it,' said Eddie. 'Slipped off his bike, apparently. Poor bastard. I wonder who he was.'

'His name was Majid,' replied Lech, 'I had a look at the flowers. According to the flowers his mates all think he was some sort of hero.'

'Fucking shame,' said Eddie, 'a young life like that wasted and all cos he slipped off his bike. There'll be plenty at his funeral.'

'Trax will miss it,' smiled Albert.

'He'll be cut up about that,' laughed Eddie.

'Yes, he'll be in pieces,' smiled Lech in a rare glimpse of the big man's gallows humour.

'He'll be all over the place,' laughed Eddie.

'Stop it, you two,' said Albert laughing.

All three were in a jovial mood when Mark joined them at the bar.

'You three seem to be in a good mood,' said Mark, 'don't tell me it was because Albert's team won on Friday night.'

'Not just that, Mark,' said Eddie, 'it looks like all these black and Asian gang members are killing each other off. There soon won't be any left. Anyway, here comes the grub. Good timing, Mark.'

'The big black who runs the gang round here,' said Mark, 'somebody was saying he seems to have disappeared.'

Albert replied, 'Yes, things have got a little bit better round here. He must have gone on holiday. I'm sure he's enjoying himself wherever he is.'

Mark couldn't help but notice the smiles on the three faces of his drinking companions.

'Another one died on Friday in a bike accident, so that's another one less to worry about, but there's still a few of them capable of making nuisances of themselves.' said Eddie.

'Nice break, Albert?' asked Mark.

'Yes, very nice, thanks, Mark. Lovely and peaceful. No yobs, clean streets. The Spanish police are obviously doing their job. Lovely warm weather. Cheaper housing than here in this shithole. It wouldn't take a lot for me to move there.'

30.

At Southgate police station Cronk assembled his troops for the five o'clock office meeting. Detective Sergeant Webster looked around the room and saw that everyone had her attention.

She said, 'The enquiry is not moving on as fast as we would like. At the Stratford end, the suspects for our murder have either disappeared or been involved in in fatal road accidents. Which could be coincidental, or not. The only suspect of note that we can concentrate on, is the Pakistani called Saf. We do not think that he has any connection to our murder at McDonald's but he is one of the main players in our investigation into the Stratford gang and the governor has authorised surveillance of Saf, hoping that he can shed some light on what has taken place. The surveillance will take place in and around the park where they do their dealing. We are not going to be proactive in respect of this minor dealing but we will attempt to build a bigger picture and profile of this individual. Overtime payments have been authorised but due to cutbacks and financial restraints these observations will be limited to the evenings Monday up until Friday evenings. Detective

Constable McEvoy, here, will be the liaison between the two sets of surveillance teams from our end and that of Forest Gate.'

Later that evening, after the office meeting finished, DS Webster and DC McEvoy, with Detective Chief Inspector Cronk sitting in one of the rear seats, drove to Forest Gate Police station to meet up with Detective Inspector David Marker. All four made themselves comfortable in Marker's office.

After the formalities of handshakes, Cronk started proceedings by addressing DI Marker,

'Dave, I have to say straight away that I am under extreme pressure from my hierarchy at Southgate who are telling me that we are running too big a squad. As you know it's the first step to closing the investigation down and just leaving a couple of personnel on it, just for the purpose of going through the motions. But, I have received permission to have a closer look at this 'Saf' individual, although typically it's not twenty-four seven coverage.'

'Bill, we are surrounded by pressure,' replied Marker, 'I'm getting it in the neck about crime stats and crime rates in this borough. Well, I was, but things have gone quiet lately and I have a lovely warm pleasant feeling in my gut that it's because one of the biggest toe rags in the area has mysteriously disappeared and one of his henchmen, very unfortunately, met his maker after an accident, whereby he broke his neck on a lamppost.'

'Oh dear,' replied Cronk, 'what a shame. Hope the lamppost wasn't damaged in any way.'

Marker replied, 'And fortunately, or unfortunately, depending on which way you look at it, there isn't a single witness to the event, save to say that a passing bus driver thought he saw a big dark saloon coming out of that turning at the time of the accident.'

Cronk replied, 'Wouldn't it be wonderful if all these types just went around killing each other off, provided no innocents were involved?'

Marker replied, 'Indeed. The only problem you've got is that there is an innocent young girl, who has got caught up in this just by being in the wrong place at the wrong time. The one thing I will say to you is that the main suspect has disappeared and that his sidekick is in the mortuary on a cold slab or in a refrigerated sliding box with an identification card attached to his big toe.'

Cronk asked, 'When you say disappeared, Dave, how permanent do you think his disappearance is?'

'Nothing concrete, although he might be wearing one of those concrete jackets,' laughed Marker at his own humour, 'but I just have a hunch that we might not see him again.'

'One of your famous hunches, Dave, and if you're right, it makes my job almost redundant. I'll report back to my Commander. He will ask me to speak to the dead girl's family. They will not be happy but might get a small piece of consolation knowing that the perpetrators are no more.'

'Bill, can I just ask one favour,' asked Marker, 'can you keep the surveillance going for a couple of weeks?'

'No problem, Dave, but it's only a part-time effort. We haven't been authorised for the full ticket.'

Proceedings were then concluded and the four officers retired to the police station annexe, more commonly known as the Bell public house, where they remained in discussion talking about their impending retirements and prospects of promotion respectively.

31.

At the back of his brother's newsagents' shop Saf sat on a pile of newspapers due to be returned to the wholesaler. He mourned the loss of his associate, Trax, because he was the prime mover as far as Saf's income was concerned and now that he had been got at by the local shits he decided that his only way forward was to come back at these middle-aged white arseholes and make them hurt bad. This would also enhance his prospects of taking control of the gang that operated within this area.

He would fix his sights on the dead dog-walker who he had heard was called Albert Oxford. He had been the one that he and Trax had put in hospital and if it hadn't been for the old bastard with the Alsation, then this 'Albert' would be lying next to Mujid in the mortuary.

'Albert' had shown him Trax's nose ring but Saf knew where Albert lived. He also suspected that the park and himself, in particular, were probably being watched by the police, so it was convenient for him to spend quite a bit of time at his brother's shop helping out here and there and using the upstairs storage room to crash out and sleep when he needed to.

Saf thought long and hard about his plan. He would only use one of the gang, a black youth called Duane, to help him in his efforts to exterminate 'Albert.'

32.

Albert was dozing peacefully in his big armchair when he was startled by the loud crash of his front room window smashing, scattering glass everywhere on the carpet. He noticed a lump of rock on the carpet and got himself away from the window. Another volley of rocks shattered what remained of the window and dragged down the net curtaining.

Albert ran to the back of the house thinking that it would be folly to attempt to leave by his street door as that was exactly what the attackers would probably be hoping for.

Instead, Albert left by his rear door and went to the back of his garden where he scaled the three-foot-high fence that separated his garden from that of Harry's. Albert could see that Harry and Libby were in the rear dining room.

Harry spotted a figure in his rear garden and immediately picked up a long-bladed meat knife from his kitchen drawer and went to the kitchen door which led out to his back garden.

'What the fuck are you doing Albert?' he said on seeing his next-door neighbour staring into his kitchen.

'There's a mob outside putting in all my windows. Can you ring the old bill for me, please?' said Albert, shaking with rage and with a modicum of fear.

'I wondered what the racket was.' Harry went to his front living room to find that his wife had already called the emergency phone number and had requested police attendance.

Within ten minutes the sound of police sirens signalled the arrival of two marked police cars. Telling Albert to remain indoors, Harry went out into the street to speak to the police officers.

'What has been happening here?' asked the sergeant in charge.

'Pretty obvious, I would have thought,' replied Harry, scornfully, 'A load of yobs have just put in the windows of my next-door neighbour's house.'

'Did you see who was responsible?'

'No.'

'Then how do you know it was a crowd of yobs?'

'My next-door neighbour saw them. Who else would do something like this?' asked Harry contemptuously.

'And why would they want to do it?' asked the sergeant. 'Why have they got a beef with your neighbour?'

'Nothing better to do, I suppose,' replied Harry, 'I'm sure if they had a game of table tennis, or a 'yoof' club to go to, none of this would have happened.'

The sergeant made it clear that he was not impressed with Harry's sarcasm and surveyed the damage. Every front facing window had been smashed, including the two upstairs bedroom windows.

'Where is your neighbour?' asked the younger police-men.

'I don't know,' replied Harry.

Harry supplied Albert's name and the police officers took their leave. Before going back indoors Harry looked up and down the street but it was like a ghost town, or one of those streets in the cowboy movies where everybody is cowering behind closed doors when the big baddie rides into town.

Back in the safety of his own house, Harry said to Albert, 'They were as much use as a chocolate teapot, but at least their presence seems to have scared them off. It's obviously that Pakistani geezer with the big hooter. I don't think he's gonna leave you alone. You're gonna have to do something about him or he'll always be trying to dig you out. He'll be like shit sticking to a blanket.'

'You are right, Harry, but in the meantime, what am I going to do at this minute?'

'Well, short term, we need to get your house secured. I'm going to ring a twenty-four hour call out emergency builder from the local paper. Then you can park up here. You can give me your house keys and I'll supervise the repair job.'

Three hours later the builders' company had finished their emergency boarding up procedure. Every shard of glass had been removed from the window frames and had been replaced with wooden ply-wood boards which had been securely battened into place.

Harry supervised the work whilst Libby made herself busy by attempting to clear up the mess in Albert's living room and bedrooms. By the time she had finished the morning dawn was not far off and the three of them convened in Harry's dining room for a pot of tea and slices of buttered toast.

'I think it would be best if you are not seen going into your house, Albert. What I suggest is that you come in by my garden side gate, jump the fence, and let yourself in by your back door to the kitchen. The less they see of you, the better.'

'Good idea, Harry. Because of the emergency boarding I can safely have the lights on and nobody will know I'm in there.'

Everything was agreed and once Albert had squared up Harry for the emergency builders, he hopped over the communal garden fence and picked up a torch from his kitchen utilities cupboard. He was dismayed to see the mess the place had been left in but was similarly impressed with the Herculean clearing-up tasks performed by the redoubtable Libby.

Albert decided that sleep was his first priority and that was made easier by the fact that there was not a chink of daylight inside his house due to the boarding up process.

33.

Albert had slept fitfully and decided to pay a visit to Eddie in The Princess Victoria. He slipped out by using the rear garden, jumping Harry's fence and letting himself out onto the street by the side gate.   The pub was fairly quiet and Albert was able to confide in Eddie what had happened during the previous evening.

'You will need to do something about him, Albert. Harry is right. This knobhead obviously knows you had something to do with Trax disappearing but I can't believe he hasn't put the bike rider's death down to me. He knows you were in the car. You need to be careful. Do you know where he lives? I would gladly come with you and put in every window in his house. I was top of the class with the grenade throwing exercises at Sandhurst.'

Albert smiled and said, 'No, unfortunately I don't know where he hangs out, Eddie, but when I do you'll be the first to know.'

Albert just had the one pint and then went back to his house using the circuitous route through Harry's back garden. When he sat down, he surveyed the remnants of the mess. What would his late wife Lizzie think of all this?

Albert mused over all of this and was now more determined than ever that he was going to exact his revenge on the Pakistani.

Albert remained inside his house for the rest of the day with the radio on at low volume listening to idiotic radio presenters spouting garbage about how they would sort out London's gangs whilst they lived a life of commuting from the safety of their leafy London suburbs into their Central London broadcasting studio. Knobheads, the lot of them!

Albert managed to salvage a meal from bits and pieces in the fridge and freezer and decided he could pass the evening listening quietly to some music. The effect of the soporific melodies sent Albert off into a fairly deep sleep. No surprise really considering what had gone on in his life the past few weeks.

Albert woke up with a start. He did not know what time it was as the room was in complete darkness. The music was still playing softly but Albert was aware of the acrid smell of smoke which caught the back of his throat.

He rushed into his hallway and saw that his street door was alight with flames licking up the wooden door frame. He could smell petrol and saw that the flames extended from the carpeted floor up to his letter box and could see that the fire had taken hold.

He raced into the kitchen and although struggling to breathe he was able to douse a hand towel and fill a plastic washing-up bowl with water. He ran back to the front door and he threw the basin of water at the flames. He flailed at them with the wet towel. This did not have the success he had hoped for and he now had to consider his escape route.

Leaving by his front street door was what his attackers would probably want so once again he had to leave by his kitchen rear door and jump into Harry's rear garden.

Albert could see that Harry and Libby were awake, Harry in shorts and T-shirt. Harry waved him in through his rear garden door.

'I've called the Fire Brigade. In the meantime, you'd better wait here at the back of the house.'

Across the road, Mo Connors watched the scene unfold through the net curtains of her upstairs bedroom window. She never missed any of the events that happened within a twenty-five-yard radius of her front garden gate.

Three fire engines attended the scene of the fire. Albert's street door was smashed open and the fire was extinguished mainly by foam appliances. Hoses were unwound as a precaution and attached to the street stopcock. Temporary signs prevented other traffic using the street. A knot of passers-by gathered to watch the Fire Brigade in action.

The firemen entered Albert's house to ensure that there were no other seats of fire and once satisfied returned to their respective fire engines to begin the process of reeling back in their respective water hoses. Two of the fire engines left the scene leaving one behind with the overall Fire Officer-in-charge. He knocked on Harry's door, 'I understand, sir, that you were the gentleman who called the Fire Brigade.'

'Yes mate, that's right. The person who lives next door is in my kitchen. You'll probably want a word.'

The Fire Officer bristled a little at being addressed as

'mate' and being told what to do but nevertheless went in to speak to Albert, not caring about his wet muddy boots leaving their imprints on Harry's nearly new carpet.

'I will need your formal permission to enter your house officially to investigate the cause of the fire.'

'Not a problem, mate, help yourself,' said Albert. 'The place is already a mess so don't bother about wiping your feet when you go in.'

Albert remained in Harry's house fortified by strong tea and the occasional nip of Harry's malt whisky.

After an hour the Fire Officer knocked and asked to speak to Albert.

'The matter will have to be reported to the police. My initial investigations with my colleague here reveals that a flammable accelerant was poured through your letterbox and was lit by a petrol-soaked rag. My colleague has taken some samples which will be handed to the police officers investigating this case of arson.'

Albert thanked the two firemen and they left in the last remaining fire-engine.

'I'm going to have to call out our emergency builder friend,' said Albert. 'He's earning a good living out of me.'

'You might want to ring the estate agent, Albert, and get the fuck out of here. You are making our street look like something out of East Beirut. And the house prices will have dropped through the floor. Good job. I don't want to leave here anytime soon.'

The rest of that night was spent in Harry's kitchen with cups of tea punctuated by catnaps. After a bacon sandwich provided by Libby Albert decided it was time to make a move. He now realised that staying in his house was a problem that would not go away until he had taken care of the cause of his problems.

He realised the opposition were fighting back. He was also putting into danger the lives of those people who lived next door to him.

As he left Harry's house he squinted through the morning sunlight to see what state his home was in. Harry was right. East Beirut it was. Every window boarded up with plywood and the front door blackened by fire. What a mess!

Albert thought about what Harry had said. He had to move away from here temporarily. He entered his house by the rear garden route and removed his stock of cash from the floor safe. The house was in a terrible state not helped by the robustness of the firemen. Every room stank of smoke and evidence of the fire was most apparent in the hallway by the front street door.

Albert took a stroll in the morning sunshine to the Princess Victoria. The pub was not open yet but Albert spotted Eddie by the rear gates, presumably readying himself for a delivery from the brewery.

'He tried to kill me last night by setting my house on fire. It's in a bit of a state and I can't stop there for obvious reasons. I need to think about a plan to get rid of Saf.'

'Are you sure it was him?' asked Eddie. 'Although, thinking about it, it can't be anyone else. If you need a hand, don't hesitate to ask.'

'My immediate problem, Eddie, is that I need somewhere to put my head down.' said Albert.

'All I've got, Albert, is a room at the top of the pub. It's a bit of an attic room. There's an old camp-bed in there. You'll need a sleeping bag and there's also a small sink. It is pretty basic but you're welcome to park yourself in there and hole up for a while.'

'Thanks Eddie,' said Albert, 'I'll take you up on that. I'll pop back to my place and get some essentials this afternoon. Cheers, mate.'

East London Gazette

The London Fire Brigade attended a house fire in the Colebrook area of Stratford on Wednesday evening and extinguished a house fire. Local Fire Chief John Abrahams told the Gazette that the incident is being treated as arson and is being dealt with by local police. Police have appealed for any possible witnesses to come forward...

After packing a holdall containing some clothing, a washbag, sleeping bag, toiletries and his mobile phone charger, Albert had a last look round the home he had shared with Lizzie for all those years. It seemed to him pretty obvious that he wouldn't be living here anymore. He would put the house on the market. He had a quick look round and saw that, apart from the charring of the door and frame, the damage seemed superficial. A new carpet would be required but otherwise the prompt attendance of the Fire Brigade had kept the damage to a minimum.

Albert made his way back to his new temporary residence. Eddie showed him upstairs to the attic room.

'As I said, Albert, it is a bit basic, but it is a roof over your head. You can duck your nut here until we sort out the immediate problem. You can get a phone signal up here and I can give you the wi-fi code to keep you abreast of things. Whatever you want to eat, just come down and order it.'

'Thanks, Eddie, I appreciate this, and hopefully it will be sorted out sooner, rather than later.'

Albert had a look round the sparsely furnitured room. No bigger than a prison cell, it at least had a view from a small window overlooking the backyard of the pub and across several rooftops and gardens.

There was a small sink, alongside which Eddie had left a clean towel and bar of soap. The towel and soap looked like Army issue. Albert smiled. He tried out the camp bed for comfort. It wasn't a five-star deluxe suite, but it would suffice.

An old wooden wardrobe which looked like it had survived the Second World war stood empty with a few bare, plastic coat-hangers, dangling from a metal rail. Albert placed his clothing neatly away and had a look out into the corridor. He was pleased to see a single-use toilet and decided he would be able to make the best of what he had until he had made a decision about what he was going to do about the troublesome Pakistani who had tried to kill him on at least two occasions.

He suddenly remembered that Detective Constable

153

McEvoy had wanted to have a chat with him. He picked up his phone and rang McEvoy's number.

'The last time I spoke to you, Mr McEvoy, you said you wanted to have a chat with me. I have been preoccupied with other matters but I can see you tomorrow if it suits you.'

'Can you be at Forest Gate Police Station at five pm? I will see you at the front counter.'

34.

After a few days of helping out in his brother's shop, Saf was trusted enough by his brother to be left on his own to serve customers. While he wasn't working, he either sat in the back room of the shop with Duane or was upstairs in his room which he used for sleeping. Saf was also giving consideration as to how he was going to exact revenge on the man probably responsible for getting rid of Trax and for indirectly causing the death of his good friend Mujid.

He had tried to force him out of his house by stoning the building and when that failed he had poured the petrol through his letter box. When he didn't come out of the front of the house he realised that he must have escaped at the back of the house and then made use of his friend with the scar who lived next door. He would also have to be catered for. But the immediate concern was for the man who had made Trax vanish into thin air.

35.

At five pm the following day, Albert presented himself at the front counter of the police station and asked for DC McEvoy. He appeared almost immediately and ushered Albert into a side office.

'It's come to our notice that you have been the subject of two separate attacks on your home, Mr Oxford. What is going on and why do you think your house has been targeted?'

'Beats me,' replied Albert, 'I was hoping you would tell me. But you probably haven't got the resources or the manpower.'

'Well, it's obvious you've upset someone. We don't think it's Trax because he has mysteriously disappeared, which leaves one, or more, of his accomplices.'

Albert shrugged. 'I don't know why you are worried about them. They are killing each other off. Sooner or later, they'll get the message and realise it's all been pointless. What I will say is that, at some stage, unless something is done, the local people will fight back and there will be mayhem on the streets. Not me, you understand, I'm a law-abiding citizen just minding my own business, having

156

the odd pint and watching my football team.'

'You'll be in line for the Nobel Peace prize at this rate. Where are you staying at the moment just in case I want to get hold of you?'

'I'm staying with a mate at a secret location. I don't want the people trying to murder me to know where I'm staying. You can contact me by phone if you need me.'

'Don't push your luck, Mr Oxford, replied McEvoy, 'some of us are on the same side as you.'

'Why would that be?' a surprised Albert asked.

'With the demise of these criminals, our crime rate reduction figures have been boosted. My Detective Inspector and I are flavour of the month with our bosses. The people in charge of handing out the pencils at New Scotland Yard are wetting themselves with excitement. That will eventually feed back to the Home Office. More power to your elbow.'

Albert looked at McEvoy quizzically before leaving the station.

36.

Albert's routine at his new bedsit did not vary much. When daylight started to pervade through the flimsy material that posed as a poor excuse for curtaining, Albert was awake. The camp bed was not comfortable but Albert found that he was able to sleep well. A quick wash was followed by a bacon sandwich delivered to his door by Eddie and on the odd occasion it was accompanied by a newspaper. Then, with his big jacket and hood up, Albert went on exploratory walks. He had no fixed purpose but used the walks to contemplate a plan of action but, until he knew the whereabouts of Saf, there was nothing he could do.

When lunchtime approached Albert made use of a greasy-spoon cafe in the High Street. It was frequented mainly by workmen, especially builders, and was situated between a betting shop and a Turkish men's hairdressers.

The cafe offered him a change of scenery, a chance to take the weight off his feet and the opportunity to strike up conversations with people other than the Army's top chef.

Albert would return to the pub mid to late afternoon and slip upstairs by the rear door. He had come to an arrangement with Josie, the barmaid, that ensured he had a couple of pints left in the hallway which he had previously paid for.

After a couple of days, Albert's walking habits became a little bit more adventurous and he left the safety of the main streets. By sticking strictly to the side streets and shadows and hidden under his hood and dark clothing, he decided it was just possible to have a look at Dogshit Park from a distance.

He approached the park from a direction he wouldn't normally use and when he was in an adjoining street he passed a dark grey van. As he walked past the van he heard the low crackle of a radio with tinny voices conversing.

Moving onwards he realised that he had unwittingly discovered a police surveillance vehicle and presumed that they were observing the park and its habitual nocturnal occupants.

Feeling emboldened by the police presence, Albert walked onwards towards the park. It was absolutely deserted with no sign of any human activity. Albert decided to cut back to the safety of the Princess Victoria. He saw Eddie at the doorway to the bar.

'No sign of him and nothing in the park, but the police are looking at the park,' said Albert.

'He'll turn up,' replied Eddie, 'a bad penny always shows up.'

37.

At the newsagents shop, Saf was in discussion with Duane, 'We are being destroyed. Police have the park covered and we can't find Mr Whitey. Our supply of gear is running dry and customers are confused, man. We need money. We need to visit the pubs that Trax used to get money from and force them to resume their payments to us.' Duane nodded in agreement.

..

In the unmarked police surveillance van, the occupants were disenchanted with life.

'We stand out like a sore thumb round here, and everybody has sussed out we are here. Nothing is happening. A waste of time. I heard a story once where one of the neighbours came out and left a tray of tea on the bonnet. I hope that's what is going to happen to us. I could murder a cuppa.'

The temperature dropped and the decision was made to return the vehicle to the police yard.

At the Princess Victoria the last stragglers of midweek customers were reluctantly draining what was left of their drinks. Eddie and Josie began to usher them outdoors and back to the warmth of their own homes. As the last customer left, Josie began to pick up the empty glasses and return them to the counter where they would be placed later in the glass washer. Tables were wiped and dried and chairs rearranged into a formal position in readiness for the next day's first arrivals.

Eddie went to the pub street door to lock it, but just as he got to the door, two hooded youths burst in with both brandishing weapons. The Asian one with the long nose was carrying a machete and the smaller West Indian type youth had a knife with a serrated six-inch blade. The Asian shouted

'No trouble, nobody gets hurt.'

Josie stood transfixed and Eddie said, 'What do you want?'

'Our friend Trax was given protection money by you. We are taking over his business. Three hundred pounds a week and nobody gets hurt. We don't set light to your pub and no customers get hurt.'

'That sounds like a great deal.' said Eddie mustering up as much sarcasm as he could inflect into his reply.

'Will twenty-pound notes be okay, or would you rather have something smaller? Or maybe you take a credit card?'

Eddie went to the till where he removed three hundred pounds. Josie eyed him quizzically but Eddie just winked at her. Eddie handed the money over to the Asian and they both very quickly left by the street door.

After they left Eddie climbed onto a chair by the street window and very carefully pulled open the heavy drape curtains. He saw both youths run for about one hundred and fifty yards before getting aboard a black and yellow motorbike and driving away.

Eddie went over to Josie and said, 'Don't worry about that, Josie. Nobody got hurt and I have a feeling that something bad is going to come their way.'

Eddie went up to the top floor and on seeing a light on in Albert's room tapped gently on the door. Letting him in, Albert asked what he wanted.

'I've just had two visitors. Your mate, the Pakistani and the black fucker. Looks like they've taken over from Trax the swimmer and I've given them three hundred pounds. They were both tooled up, but I see them run down the road and jump on a black and yellow motorbike. They waited until the pub had cleared. They've probably got a rota of pubs, so I reckon we can expect another visit about the same time next week.'

'Well done, Eddie,' Albert replied, 'but whatever plans we make, I insist that I will be the one who takes him out.'

'Not a problem with me, Albert. I'll bring up a little present for you and you can decide what you want to do with it.'

38.

The following morning as Albert returned from the toilet at the end of the corridor, he noticed that a small parcel lay at the foot of his room door. Measuring roughly one foot long by nine inches wide, Albert picked it up. It was heavier than he thought and on removing the outer brown wrapping paper he saw that it contained a plain wooden box with no markings. A small metal clasp held the lid securely and when Albert released the clip he opened the lid to find that the box contained a handgun.

Albert placed the box and contents below his camp bed and went down to the bar to seek out Eddie. Eddie was at the far end of the bar behind the counter sitting on his stool. The pub was bereft of clientele due to the early hour and the inclement weather outside the warmth of the saloon bar.

'You got your little pressie, then, Albert?'

'Yes, Eddie. Where did that come from?'

'Ex-army, of course. They don't use these anymore. It is old army stock. A Browning, capable of getting rid of scroats, also a couple of magazines of nine-millimetre ammunition. The Army has replaced these as standard issues with Glocks but these Brownings got the job done. They came in handy for me when I was in the Middle East.'

Albert rolled his eyes.

'I've never fired one before, Eddie,' said Albert.

'Not a problem Albert. My brother-in-law has a small holding down in Kent. We'll have a little day out down there and help him keep on top of his rabbit population. I've got extra ammunition tucked away. Maybe Lech fancies a day out and he can run us down there. I'll ring Lech and he can meet us here at midday and we'll have a talk about it. In the meantime, I'll ring my brother-in-law and fix up a visit.'

Albert retired back to his room and had a good look at the weapon. Besides the extra ammunition clips there was an oily cloth which Albert presumed had been used to clean and maintain the weapon. The handgun felt comfortable in the palm of his hand. It gave Albert a sense of power and he looked forward to getting acquainted with this newfound toy.

When Albert went downstairs to the bar the big figure of Lech was already at the bar tucking into his first pint of the day.

'I hear we go for a picnic in the country tomorrow, Albert.'

'I don't know about a picnic, Lech, but hopefully a bit of fun and some fresh air away from all this shit here.'

Arrangements were made between the three men to leave the pub about nine the next morning. They hoped to get to the smallholding by about eleven. A couple of hours shooting rabbits or tin cans and then a return to the Princess Victoria to further discuss their plan to get rid of Saf.

39.

The next morning it dawned bright and breezy. Albert had not slept well because of a mixture of excitement and anticipation of events further down the line.

A mug of tea sufficed as a substitute for breakfast and when Eddie shouted up the stairs he gathered his box and contents and made his way to the back yard where Lech and his van had been admitted to the rear yard.

Just under two hours later the van, driven by Lech and directed by the Army's finest Pioneer Corps, pulled up outside a large square bungalow. The long driveway up to the house had fencing on either side and attached to the house was a chicken run completely enclosed by fine wire fencing. They were met by a tall skinny middle-aged man dressed in dungarees.

'Hello Eddie, long time no see. How's that lovely wife of yours?'

'As beautiful as ever,' lied Eddie, being careful not to insult Billy's sister.

'I can always tell when you are lying, Eddie. 'Your lips move. Now, do you three want anything to eat?'

'No thanks, Billy, we would like to crack on. Maybe a

cup of tea before we return home.'

Billy led the three of them past the chicken coop into a large field. They skirted round the outside of the field and jumped over a style at the far end into a clearing just inside a copse of trees.

'You can see some cans and bottles on those tree stumps over there. Help yourself and if you manage to get any rabbits it will be a bonus.'

'What about the noise?' asked Albert.

'We are miles from anyone,' replied Billy, 'and if they heard anything they would know that I shoot rabbits and rats.'

Eddie thought to himself that they had their own rat to get rid of.

'I'll leave you to it, then,' said Billy. 'You'll be able to find your own way back, I presume?'

'No problems, Billy, I was the Army's top scout in the field.'

Billy rolled his eyes and smiled at the other two and started to make his way back to his bungalow.

Once he had gone Eddie produced a bag containing clips of nine-millimetre ammunition. He expertly loaded a clip into the magazine and released the safety catch.

'My advice Albert, is to hold the gun with two hands.' Eddie took up a semi crouching position with both hands on the weapon.

'The reason for that is to provide a steadying influence on the firearm and that, coupled with the fact that there is a certain amount of recoil or kickback when you fire, will help to stabilise your position.'

Eddie then put into practice what he had just told Albert and took careful aim at an empty coke can sitting on the trunk. From about twelve metres the first two missed, but not by much, whilst the third attempt sent the can cartwheeling through the air. Albert was surprised that the noise of the shots was not as loud as he had expected.

'Your turn, Albert. The safety catch is on but be careful not to point the gun at anybody unless you mean it.'

Carefully taking the handgun, Albert placed both hands on the stock. He gently released the safety catch, keeping his trigger finger outside of the trigger shield. He looked down the line of both sights and slipped his fore finger inside the guard and slowly squeezed the trigger.

Albert was surprised by the sound and also by the kick-back and recoil from the weapon and contrived to miss the tree trunk altogether. However, that was the last mishap with the gun as Albert now anticipated both noise and recoil.

The next three attempts hit the tree trunk and the last two were successful in hitting the cans.

'Remember Albert, when you are actually doing it for real you won't be shooting from twelve metres, you will be closer and you'll be able to smell his fear. He'll probably shit himself as well.'

'Thanks for that, Eddie.'

'Do you want to have a go, Lech,' Albert asked the big Pole.

Lech carefully took hold of the handgun and aimed at an empty wine bottle. The surprise element of the recoil made him miss the intended target by some distance. Lech quickly handed the weapon back to Eddie

'As my old granny used to say, you couldn't hit a cow's arse with a banjo,' said Eddie.

'Is this an English expression, Eddie?' queried Lech.

Eddie's orienteering skills got them back to Billy's bungalow and after a mug of tea the three men departed the small holding and set off for east London.

Once back inside the warmth of the saloon bar, Eddie, Lech and Albert sat away from the punters surrounding the heat of the fake log fire.

A makeshift plan was discussed. Albert would attempt to intercept Saf on his way to collect the protection money he had promised to return to collect. They agreed that it was not a certainty that Saf would return at exactly the same time and day of the week but that he would probably arrive from roughly the same direction and, in all probability, aboard the motor bike being driven by his accomplice.

It was decided, therefore, that Albert would plot himself up near to where the bike had been parked previously and Albert would confront him as Saf made his way to the Public House.

Adjacent to where they hoped the bike would be parked was an alleyway leading to a tower block of flats. Once Albert had completed his task he would exit by the alleyway. At the other end of the alleyway Lech would be waiting in his trusty van, ready and prepared to make the successful getaway.

Albert bought a round of drinks and retired to his room at the top of the building. The exertions of the day had taken it out of him and it was not long before Albert drifted off into a sleep only disturbed by the occasional sounds of raucous laughter from downstairs in the bar.

40.

The Southgate murder squad surveillance team were gradually getting more and more disenchanted with the task of watching the park for non-existent activities, so it came as a relief when Detective Sergeant Webster informed the team leader that their watchful spell in east London was coming to an end. DS Webster took it upon herself to ring Detective Inspector Marker to inform him personally.

'I can understand that decision, Elaine. In fact, I was about to ring your man to tell him that things were moving in a different direction and at a different speed. How are things going at your end with the Tottenham gang?'

'The scroats of Black Lightning seem to have gone a little quiet. It's almost as if they have realised that they were being watched. It may be that they stumbled across our surveillance team at the park on your manor. I don't like it when I don't know what they are doing or what they are up to.'

41.

The Tottenham crew had been stewing for quite some time. There was unrest in their ranks. The troops were upset that one of their friends had been gunned down in broad daylight in McDonalds. It was a recurring theme at their meetings, held below the three-lane North Circular bridge.

Revenge would have to be exacted on the perpetrators. A plan was drawn up to deal with the Stratford element who killed their associate. Weapons were retrieved from their respective hiding places and much discussion took place over the movements of the intended target; the Pakistani called Saf.

They had discovered that Saf had moved, more or less permanently, into his brother's newsagents shop and was ensconced there during daylight hours. It appeared that he slept there as well, and the only time he moved out of the shop was in the evening to conduct his criminal enterprises.

The Tottenham hierarchy was aware that by getting rid of Saf, it would solve a few problems. At the top of the list was revenge for their own friend, Joshua. It would restore their street credibility.

Saf's demise could lead to a breakup of that Stratford crew which, in turn, would open the door for the Tottenham gang to spread their own parameters for dealing drugs and making illicit profits from other various criminal activities.

42.

The following afternoon Albert Oxford met up with his big Polish friend, Lech. They left the pub together and made their way on foot to where they anticipated Saf and the rider of the motorbike would leave his motorbike, as they had done previously.

They walked up the hundred-yard alleyway surrounded on either side by eight-foot brick walls separating two large tower blocks. At the end of the alleyway, they walked out onto a roadway which served as access to the concrete jungle they now found themselves in.

'I will be waiting here with the van,' said Lech, 'and then we drive to the main road and away. We leave it sometime and then you go back to the pub,' said the Pole in his best pigeon English.

'I can't see what could possibly go wrong,' ventured Albert, although the slightly worried look on his face belied his apparent confidence.

43.

Later that afternoon below the North Circular Road close to Edmonton, criminal preparations were being made in a lock-up garage that contained three vehicles and two motor bikes. One of the vehicles, a three-year-old Vauxhall, which had just previously been stolen, had been fitted with false number plates by one of the gang who was noted for his expertise with anything to do with motor vehicles. He was also the designated driver in the venture that lay before them later that evening.

His two accomplices, who would travel with him, ensured that they had the weapons needed to deal with Saf and anybody else for that matter who may be keeping company with him. The weapons were placed under some spare matting in the boot of the red Vauxhall.

Once the finishing touches and last-minute checks had been completed, the three members of Black Lightning got into the car and set off at a sedate pace in order not to attract the attention of any law enforcement agents. They travelled in the direction of east London.

44.

Although Albert did not think that Saf would come calling for cash that night, he had agreed with Eddie and Lech that they would cover the intended route just in case Saf decided to visit Eddie earlier than expected.

The weather had turned Arctic so Eddie had provided Albert with his old Army issue greatcoat, a garment of ample proportions, which would provide warmth as well as huge pocket-space in which to conceal the firearm before any possible use.

The large greatcoat stretched down below Albert's knees and with the collar turned up and keeping to the shadows he hoped to escape being noticed by any of the locals.

He spoke with Lech on his mobile phone and told him that he was going to be in or near the alleyway from about 9pm. Lech assured him he would be at the other end of the alleyway waiting for him to appear.

As Albert stepped out into the night through the rear garden exit of the public house, the evening air was chilly and Albert was pleased that he had this huge grey Army-issue coat to keep him warm.

45.

Saf sat at the back of the shop drinking from a can of Coke. His brother was about to close the shop for the end of that day's business. Saf texted his friend, Duane, and five minutes later a dark clad figure wearing a crash helmet arrived outside the shop. Saf touched knuckles with him as a sign of greeting. He picked up and put on the crash helmet contained in the pillion box and both rode off with Duane excessively revving the bike's throttle.

..

The Black Lightning gunship cruised around the park but saw that it was deserted. The driver, a small runt of an individual, informed his fellow gang members that he was going to cruise around the local streets slowly, so as not to draw attention to the vehicle.

..

Twenty yards away from the main road where the motor bike had been spotted last week, Albert found cover by a door that led to flights of stairs and non-working lifts that belonged to the tallest tower block.

The doorway provided much needed shelter from the biting wind. Albert stood there wondering if there would be any show from Saf and his motorbike rider.

After waiting for about an hour Albert was thinking of abandoning his position when he heard the low throaty roar of an approaching motor bike. He tensed, listening to the growl of the engine. It was definitely approaching in his general direction.

The motorbike cruised to a halt. Two youths dismounted and the bike was pulled back onto its stand by the kerb. Saf was wearing a long hoodie and after stowing his helmet in the rear pannier of the bike, he pulled up his hood so that all that was visible was eyes, mouth and his long nose.

He adjusted his clothing so that he could gain access to the weapon he was carrying. His fellow passenger was wearing a dark grey puffer jacket and before they moved off as a pair, he ensured that the small blade he carried was secure and unopened in his jacket pocket, ready to be opened if and when required at the premises they were about to pay a visit to.

46.

The Tottenham gunship quietly trawled the streets of the area. They were helped by the fact that, because of the bitterly cold weather, there was not much traffic or many pedestrians braving the elements.

The attention of the front seat passenger was suddenly drawn to two dark figures dismounting from a motorbike. Parking the car carefully, the two passengers retrieved the tools they intended to use in the act of seeking revenge for their dead colleague.

The boot of the vehicle was sprung open by the driver and from below the matting the two passengers retrieved two handguns which were placed respectively into the waistband of their denim jeans and hidden from sight by the puffer jackets which seemed to be the accepted uniform. Black expensive trainers completed their outfits.

The two gunmen left the driver of the car behind the steering wheel of the car, and both youths crept towards what appeared to be the intended route of the motor bike youths. They were careful to use parked cars as cover, ducking below the height of the stationary vehicles.

··

Albert walked the short distance to intercept Saf and his accomplice. He kept his hand on the Browning and in the space provided by the huge pocket he was able to slip off the safety catch. He gripped the firearm carefully and approached the Pakistani. He was about ten yards away from the two of them and he could see in Saf's eyes a bewildered look.

Saf and his friend came to a sudden stop. Albert still had the weapon concealed. A smile developed on the face of Saf and he sneered, 'Well, look who it is. Old dog lover himself.' He opened his jacket to reveal that, held by a belt, was a scabbard from which he withdrew a machete measuring some eighteen inches in length.

'Is that the best you can do?' sneered Albert, 'You're fucking pathetic. You are a fucking disgrace.'

Saf's elongated nostrils flared, and raising the machete, approached Albert, wielding the weapon above his head. Albert now thought it was high time to reveal his own weapon but in an effort to remove the gun from his pocket the front sight snagged on the cloth lining of the pocket. Albert couldn't believe it. Was this how it was going to end?

Saf raised his weapon to strike Albert when a gunshot rang out disturbing the peace of the night.

··

The Tottenham crew, using their cover well, were now within fifteen yards of the motorbike pair. There was also

180

this big bear-like figure wearing a huge oversized coat standing in front of them. The Pakistani had a long machete in his hand and was appearing to attempt to strike the bear who was struggling with something in his pocket.

The lead Tottenham attacker swiftly took aim and put a bullet through the temple of Saf who crumpled to the ground. His associate started to run but was fired on by the other Tottenham crew member.

The first shot hit the West Indian in the thigh and he stumbled onto the roadway.

The leader of the attackers went across to him and pumped a bullet into his neck. The entry wound was fairly neat but on exiting through the spinal cord had left a gaping hole on the other side of his neck. His blood seeped slowly into the gutter.

..

Albert, in a state of shock, had now managed to extract his Browning from his pocket and held it out of sight from the two assassins.

He raised the gun and pointed it at the one who looked in charge. Using both hands as advised by Eddie, he fired twice in quick succession into the body of the youth. His scream would have woken up the dead. Well, perhaps not, in the case of the two already lying in the street.

Surprised at how quickly he was thinking he turned the gun on the other youth. He was pointing his weapon at Albert. Both guns were fired simultaneously.

Albert saw the flash of his opponent's weapon and felt

pain immediately in his right shoulder. He saw, however, that his shot had struck the gunman full square in his face which surprised Albert, as he had been aiming at the centre of his chest.

Albert clutched at the pain in his shoulder. His right arm was throbbing. Despite the excruciating pain, he placed the gun back into his right-hand pocket and shuffled towards the alleyway.

The night was eerily still. As Albert made his way down the alleyway he glanced upwards at the towering mass of concrete forming the tower blocks. No movements, no noise.

At the end of the alley-way Albert emerged into a well-lit concourse and saw to his relief, the big van with his friend the Pole sitting behind the wheel.

Lech spotted Albert once he had emerged from the alley and noticed that he seemed awkward in his movements. He left the van and opened the sliding door. Silently, he ushered Albert into the back of the van. Lech resumed his position and drove off slowly. The fifteen-minute journey was made in silence.

Lech parked the van amongst other trade vehicles in the business park at Beckton. He switched off the lights and joined Albert in the back of the van. He closed the door and switched on the interior light and saw Albert slumped amongst a pile of cloths and other cleaning materials. Albert was conscious.

'What happened, Albert?' asked Lech

'Four dead, one wounded. I've been hit in the shoulder. I didn't kill Saf or his mate. They got whacked by some other gunmen. Did you hear anything, Lech?'

'I heard the popping but it didn't sound that loud. I heard a scream.'

'That was the big girl Saf, breathing his last, I'm pleased to say.'

'We need to get a look at you, Albert. First thing is we need to get that coat off.'

Albert had to endure severe physical pain whilst the Pole tried as gently as he could to remove the greatcoat.

Albert had been hit at the top of his right shoulder and although there was a good deal of blood, Lech was able to staunch the flow with the use of his cleaning cloths.

'Looks like only a flesh wound, Albert. The big coat probably saved you.'

'When we get back to the pub I'll let the Army's champion First Aider have a look at it and get me patched up. The big problem I've got is how to tell him his Sunday best coat is ruined.'

47.

Marvin Clarke was now in a quandary. He had heard the gunshots and when his two compatriots from the Black Lightning gang did not reappear, he feared the worst.

He couldn't abandon the vehicle and there was the extra problem that in the compartment by the driver's door was a Glock pistol loaded with ammunition. He thought about his situation and decided that to stay near the sound of the gunshots was asking for trouble. He did not want to be implicated.

He started the engine and moved slowly away and prepared to make a slow drive back towards the Tottenham area where he would abandon the car and set light to it in an effort to get rid of incriminating evidence left in the car.

Clarke drove towards Leabridge Road and as he turned into the thoroughfare which would lead him to Upper Clapton and Tottenham, he suddenly noticed that in front of him were two marked police cars with blue flashing lights whirling in the blackness of the night. He braked and went to reverse into the turning he had just left but saw in the rear-view mirror two more flashing lights approaching from behind. The only alternative was to turn right onto Leabridge Road. But, immediately, the four police cars set off after him in pursuit.

Clarke attempted to distance himself from his pursuers. At this time of night there was not a lot of moving traffic. Clarke was struggling to get any sort of distance between him and his pursuers. He jumped a red light and immediately turned left. He was dismayed to see that approaching him was another marked police car with flashing blue lights.

The approaching car came to a stop some two hundred yards in front of him and positioned itself across the road. Due to the parked cars in the street, this cut off any chance of Clarke progressing. The police cars behind were gaining ground quickly. Clarke stopped his car. He grabbed the Glock pistol and left the car. He ran in the direction of a bus stop and could see that behind the stop was an area of grass with a children's playground containing some swings, a seesaw and a small roundabout.

He heard a booming voice on a tannoy telling him to stop. He looked round and saw that two of the police officers were armed. He raised his gun and pointed it at the two police officers. Clarke's body was hit with a fusillade of five bullets.

His body fell onto the roundabout. The roundabout spun round in slow motion with the lifeless body of Clarke lying draped grotesquely across the structure.

..

Lech rang Eddie at the Princess Victoria.

'I've got Albert in the van. He's been hit, but he's okay. What's happening at your end?'

'Nothing much. Four bodies and World War 3 would be quieter than this. There are police everywhere. You won't be able to bring him back here tonight. The place is swarming with police and television crews. How bad has Albert been hurt?'

'Not too bad. Flesh wound on his right shoulder. What he needs is a good paramedic, army trained, to patch him up.'

'Haha, that'll be me. If you take care of him tonight I'll try to get to him tomorrow and do one of my special repair jobs.'

'Okay Eddie, I will take care of him tonight and get him to you in the morning.'

Lech relayed the gist of the conversation to Albert, omitting the part where Eddie had said he would do a special job on Albert.

'The place is alive with police and press, Albert, so tonight I take the van to my place and you sleep in the back of the van until morning. Then we get you back to the pub and Eddie looks after you.'

48.

BBC News, ITN, Channel 4 News

Last night in a devastating outbreak of violence, four youths were gunned down in East London. All four victims were pronounced dead at the scene. The names of the dead are being withheld until their families have been notified. An unofficial police source said that the incident was thought to be gang related...

Walthamstow Recorder

An armed seventeen-year-old youth was shot dead by armed police last night near Blackhorse Road Tube Station. An unofficial police source said that this incident was probably linked to the deaths of four other men in Stratford last night...

East London Gazette

After a night of violence in Stratford last night, police are attempting to put together the pieces of the jigsaw which led to the carnage. Local publican Eddie Baines said 'It's very sad what is happening to this area. People are trying to get on quietly with their lives, minding their own business when all of this is happening. It takes me back to my days in the Army serving in the Middle East'...

School mums delivering their young children to the local primary school had to pick their way carefully between assorted television crews, cameras and cables.

A well-dressed reporter with a clipboard stood ready to broadcast what information he had to the breakfast television channel. He was attended to by a cameraman and sound man holding a long fluffy microphone. He was one of six television crews.

The street was closed to traffic and the roadway was littered with yards of cable connecting the nation to the scene. A helicopter hovered in the sky. Some two hundred yards away the reporter pointed at four red and white striped plastic tents which had been erected to cover the bodies of the four dead youths. White plastic suited forensic officers attended the scene.

Plain clothes policemen were everywhere and had just started to commence their house-to-house enquiries but they knew that this would be a complete waste of time as traditionally the locals said nothing, either through a misplaced sense of loyalty to the perpetrators, or because they feared recriminations if they got involved in any way.

Eddie prepared the pub for what he hoped would be a busy day. A host of media people, plain clothes policemen and local dignitaries might pay him a visit. He hoped the Mayor of London would pop in. He'd give him a piece of his mind. He'd tell him that this part of London was lawless and he'd ask him what he was going to do about all the criminals in the area.

By the time darkness had started to descend, the camera crews had left. Four tents still remained in position. Police tape had made the street a no-go area and there was a uniformed presence guarding the scene.

The figure of a man in dark clothing clutching his shoulder approached the rear gates of the Princess Victoria. The gates were opened with a minimum of noise by a rotund figure and the dark shape slipped into the back yard and went up the stairs of the pub to the top floor.

Albert was followed up the stairs to his temporary abode by Eddie. Once inside his room Eddie got to work on Albert's flesh wound. It was cleaned and bandaged.

'No damage done,' said Eddie, 'just take it easy for a few days. You've caused quite a stir around here. I thought you were just going to top the Pakistani.'

'That was the intention,' Albert replied, 'but these other fuckers just showed up and it was like something out of the OK Corral.'

'What's happened to my best coat?' Eddie asked.

'It's ruined, Eddie, sorry. It's got some blood on it and a bullet hole through the shoulder, but knowing you, you'll be quite happy to wear it.'

'Where is it now?' smiled Eddie, 'and what about the shooter?'

'They're with Lech and he's going to get rid of them. He's probably already done it by now. I'm sure the coat will be given a burial with full military honours,' smiled Albert.

49.

Two days later Detective Inspector Marker and Detective Constable McEvoy attended Southgate Police station to pay a social visit to Detective Chief Inspector Cronk.

The three officers met up in the glass bowl that served as Cronk's office overseeing the computer operators in the main murder squad office. The levels of activity had decreased markedly since the squad was first set up to investigate the killing of Marcia Williams and the Black Lightning gang member.

'How about I take you out for a bit of liquid lunch?' Cronk said to the two visiting detectives.

'Okay by me, Bill. We need to have a chat about where we're at,' replied Marker.

McEvoy drove the two senior men to a large sprawling pub set back off the main road leading north out of London towards Cambridge. The pub was not busy despite the fact that it had a reputation for good homely food and a decent pint.

McEvoy brought over two pints of ale, restricting himself to a tonic water as he was the designated driver. Not that he had much choice in the matter.

'How is your enquiry going?' Marker asked Bill Cronk.

'It's not going anywhere, Dave, both killers have been taken care of from what I understand. One is definitely in the morgue and your man here, young John McEvoy, tells me that Trax, the other suspect, has disappeared permanently. I have been placed under financial pressure to wind things up. I know the identity of the two killers. I can write that into the report and I can tell the family of the poor young dead girl that I am satisfied about the identity of her killers and that they no longer exist. And good riddance too!'

Marker nodded and replied, 'So you will be closing down your squad?'

'I'll keep on a couple of skeleton staff just to tidy things up and do the report. That will probably be my lot. My family has been on to me for ages to pack it in. My health is not all that great either. What about your end of town?' asked Cronk.

'Well, our patch resembled a film set from a war movie and the place is crawling with the brains from Scotland Yard who have taken up the enquiry into the killings. It would appear, though, that they are thinking along the lines that it was just an outbreak of severe violence between your Tottenham mob and the shits from our neck of the woods. I am quite happy to go along with that line of thinking for now. The only worry I have is that I am pretty sure that Tottenham had nothing to do with the disappearance of Trax. A bonus for us is that, apart from the shootings, ordinary reported crime is way down and that reflects well on me and my staff.'

The ordered sandwiches arrived and pleasantries other than crime discussions were exchanged.

Cronk was dropped back at Southgate after lunch and on the way back to Forest Gate Police Station Marker said to McEvoy, 'I have my own theories about Trax but between you and me John, I'm not too fussed about doing anything about it. If these fuckers want to go about killing each other then, so be it.'

'What about Trax?' asked McEvoy

'I think we will let sleeping dogs lie,' answered Marker before lapsing into a snooze in the front seat of the car.

50.

Albert Oxford had spent most of the next few days after the shootings holed up in his attic room at the Princess Victoria. He reflected on what had happened. How had his mundane, peaceful, enjoyable routine of life descended into this?

What had been his happy marital home with Lizzie was now a monument to the failing of the community to bind the people together. If he had been left alone, none of this would have happened.

Eddie faithfully attended Albert every day to attend to his dressings. The wound seemed to be healing remarkably quickly which allowed Albert to resume his morning walks to the greasy-spoon cafe and partake of a decent breakfast.

He listened carefully to the conversations between the builders and plasterers and all agreed that it was a good thing that these gangsters had been removed from the streets.

Once replenished, he decided it was time to show his face in the bar. The pub saloon bar was packed, not just with regulars, but with a smattering of journalists still trying to squeeze out a story for their hungry editors.

Eddie was parked in prime position sitting on his favourite high backed stool at the end of the bar holding court, with his audience hanging on every word about his adventures fighting the Irish Republican Army in Belfast or fronting up against the Taliban in the deserts of the Middle East. Eddie was bought a constant supply of beer and this encouraged him to keep going. He was rapidly evolving into the Princess Victoria's very own war correspondent.

Albert sat down in one of the comfy chairs. Eddie came across with a pint.

'Well, if it isn't Kate Adey of ITN. Thanks Eddie,' said Albert.

'You look deep in thought, Albert.'

'Eddie, I've had enough of being around here. I'm going to move to Spain. Better quality of life and warm weather. This has become a third-world country around here. I'm going to put my place on the market, accept a price, probably a lot less than it's worth, and rent Ray's brother's place until I can find a place of my own after my house sale goes through.'

'Bloody hell, Albert, that's a big step. Though when I think about it, it's not a bad idea. You've got no ties here. I'm lumbered with this place and her upstairs.'

Albert finished his pint and decided to pay his next-door neighbour, Harry, a courtesy call. The crime scene that he had caused was now open for business again. Although he walked in broad daylight he shuddered when he passed the alley that had served as an escape route. He realised he had been lucky, not just in surviving being shot at and hit, but also by a contrivance of circumstances where both police and the media seemed to be assuming that the shootout was entirely gang related.

Albert knocked on Harry's door. He answered with a smile.

'Come in mate, you've been busy. I heard from Lech that you had been winged. How are you?'

'I'm okay, Harry. I just wanted to let you and Libby know that I'm putting up next door for sale. I am going to be in Spain for a while at Ray's brother's place while my place gets sold. I won't get the going rate but I don't care. I need to get away from all this shit. I'm not sleeping well and I want a bit of quality of life before it's too late. Sorry if it looks like I'm abandoning the sinking ship.'

'No, mate, you're doing the right thing. Libby and I were talking about selling up as well. She's been on at me for years to move down to near her sister's in Southend. I won't miss this area. It's a fucking mess. The only thing I'll miss is the crew at the meat market but then Libby said I can always go up by train once a month and she can go shopping in London.'

'Sounds like a plan, Harry. Hope it works out.' Albert and Harry hugged awkwardly, as grown middle-aged men do, and left his neighbour on his doorstep.

Albert walked across the road to Mo Connor's house. She eventually answered at the third time of ringing and appeared in her usual dowdy attire. She did not say anything but just looked at Albert, expressionless.

'I'm sorry about everything that has gone on around here, Mo, but I have decided to move on. I am putting my house up for sale and I am moving to Spain. This area has gone downhill and I need to get away.'

'I don't blame you. If I was younger I would probably do the same but I have been here for years. God only knows what sort of people will move into your place.'

Albert didn't think it was an opportune time to tell her that she was also going to lose Harry as a neighbour. He would leave that to him. Albert bade farewell to the old woman and walked to the house of his big Polish friend, Lech.

Albert sat down on one of Lech's comfortable armchairs.

'Krupnik, Albert?' asked Lech

'No, definitely not,' replied Albert. 'I have come round to tell you, that it is with much sadness that I have to tell you I am selling up and I intend to settle down in Spain.'

'Albert, these people have a lot to answer for. Everybody was getting along nicely and now all this has happened. I am not staying here.'

'What are you going to do, Lech? Where will you go?'

'As you know, Albert, Annelka and I cannot have children. I will sell my business and my house and we will move back to a village in Poland and we will adopt children.'

Albert was upset at this piece of information and did his best to hide his emotions.

'Look what they have done to us. The area is a ghetto. It's going to get worse and we're being hounded out of our homes. They have a lot to answer for. I'm glad six of them are dead. I'm sorry, Lech.'

'Albert, we tried to fight back but it looks as if they have won in the end. We are all going our separate ways.'

'Yes, that is true, Lech, but we are alive and you and Annelka will bring up beautiful children. You, and they, will have a better quality of life. Nobody here has looked after our interests. And it's not just happening in this area. It's happening all over London and in all the big cities up and down the country.'

51.

Albert Oxford spent the next few days tidying up as many loose ends as possible. He visited his house which had a six-foot tall 'For Sale' sign firmly planted in the front garden. He packed clothes that he would take to Spain and in the back room he arranged items which would be placed in storage.

He had a last, lingering look round, remembering the happier times he had shared with Lizzie. They were all now in the distant past.

Harry offered him a lift to the Princess Victoria with his bags. A short-term rental of Ray's brother's apartment had been arranged whilst Albert sought to secure a property of his own in Spain. The difference between the respective housing markets in the two countries, plus the fact that Albert was downsizing considerably, meant that Albert would have a fair sum of money with which to survive.

When the day arrived, Albert could not bring himself to see Harry and Lech. After he had ordered his minicab to the airport he went down to the bar.

'Private Eddie Baines. The British Army's finest. It has been an honour to know you. I will miss you and your kindness, your hospitality and your sense of humour. Look after yourself, Eddie.'

'Everybody is leaving, Albert,' said Eddie, welling up. 'It'll be like Rorke's Drift round here. Take care, enjoy the sunshine and send us the odd postcard.'

After another awkward man-hug, Albert left by the front street door and got into the waiting cab.

52.

The Ryanair plane floated gently onto the runway at Alicante airport. Albert looked out of his porthole window and could see the shimmering heat haze. He already felt that he had made the right decision.

A taxi took him to Charlie's apartment where he would stay until he had negotiated buying a place of his own.

After unpacking, he took a walk into the small coastal town and made appointments for the next day to see an English-speaking solicitor and a similarly disposed linguist in a local Spanish estate agents. Albert knew that there had already been interest in his old home, especially at the knockdown asking price.

..

For the next two weeks, life resumed into Albert's normal routine of walks, fresh air, a glass or two of alcohol, Mediterranean food and restful sleep.

His London based solicitor informed him by telephone that an offer had been made on his house and that the purchasers were keen to tie up the deal.

Two days later his Spanish estate agent called him to say that there were three properties available for viewing. All three were situated in the town and two of them were a very short walk from the seafront.

The next day the estate agent picked Albert up. They travelled in his saloon car to view the properties. The first property was very dingy and situated in a back street. The sound of dogs barking put Albert off immediately.

The second property that was viewed fitted the bill perfectly. Situated in a quiet, tree-lined street, the property consisted of a first floor two-bedroom apartment. It was in a decent state of repair apart from some work which was needed on the bathroom and shower. A small kitchen and bar led off a fair-sized living room which would eventually house Sky television, WiFi and some air conditioning.

The bonus was the balcony, which was accessible through French windows in the living room. The balcony had views across the rooftops and this vista led to the bright blue sea, speckled with sailing craft of all shapes and sizes.

A parking space at street level also came with the property. Albert decided there and then that this was the place for him. A fairly big profit would be realised between the sale of his east London home and the acquisition of his Spanish apartment.

..

Two weeks later Albert had taken up occupancy of his new home. His time was taken up with organising and supervising the repairs and alterations he wanted carried out. He was helped in this respect by the fact that there were in abundance a host of expatriates who were skilled in the type of job Albert wanted carried out. An added bonus of these arrangements was that by paying cash the work was considerably cheaper. The plumber who installed the new shower unit asked Albert if he intended to find work in Spain.

'My lack of Spanish hampers me a bit but I think I will need to do something to occupy my time.'

'I've got the perfect job for you,' the plumber replied. 'There is a car rental place in town that is looking for drivers. All you will be doing is taking a car to the airport for incoming holidaymakers and businesspeople. When their car hire period is over you then take the car back to the car hire depot. It keeps you ticking over and invariably all the customers will speak English.'

'Sounds good, thanks,' said Albert.

The following day Albert attended the car hire firm and on production of his passport, driving licence and proof of address he was signed up as a driver.

His next port of call was to a small building in a narrow street behind the main shopping area. This office advertised Spanish speaking lessons. Albert signed up for a twice weekly evening class.   Now that Albert was in the mood he made his next move and that was to visit a second-hand car dealer. A price was negotiated on a ten-year-old Berlingo van which would serve as a runaround.

Albert drove the Berlingo to his new Spanish home and

reflected that after all this business he was going to spoil himself with a glass of Rioja. He sat on the balcony lapping up the last of the sun's rays before it dipped below the rooftops and the sea. He reflected on how his life had changed dramatically in the last few weeks. East London seemed centuries ago.

53.

Tottenham Mercury

Detective Chief Inspector William Cronk retired from the Metropolitan Police yesterday after a long and distinguished career, He told the Mercury that the fight against crime would be more difficult due to Government and local council cuts and warned that it was likely that the local population might fight back in the form of vigilantes if the problem was not addressed in the near future...

'**H** *ola, ¿cómo te va,* Albert?'

Albert looked up and couldn't believe what he was seeing. Standing in front of him was the well-dressed figure of Mark, who Albert had never seen other than in the Princess Victoria at Sunday lunch times. Mark was smartly dressed as normal except that he was not wearing a jacket but had his shirt sleeves rolled down and buttoned at the cuff.

'Well, this is a surprise, Mark, what are you doing here? I take it this is not a coincidence?'

'It's not, Albert. I need to speak to you about what has been going on in the UK.'

'It's ok, I've got English television out here and that little newspaper shop over there sells English newspapers.'

'It would be better, Albert, if you were not so flippant. You and I need to sit down and have a chat. I have some official business to attend to, but let's meet up this afternoon and we can talk about your future.'

'What the fuck are you on about, Mark. I'm sitting here minding my own business in the Spanish sunshine and along you pop, telling me what's going to happen. You're making me feel very uncomfortable.'

'This is my mobile number. Give me a ring after lunch.' With that he handed over a plain card with a phone number on it. Nothing else, just a series of numbers.

Mark walked off along the seafront. Albert paid for his coffee and considered what had just happened. What did Mark want? Why was he here in Spain? How did he find me? All sorts of questions raced through Albert's scrambled brain. Was his idyllic lifestyle here in Spain about to end before it had really begun?

Albert walked back to his flat mulling over the shock of his surprise visitor. He stopped at an electrical hardware shop and in his fractured Spanish was able to make a purchase.

Albert sat on his small balcony and took in the shimmering view of the sea. Whatever Mark had come to see him about he didn't want to swap this view for any other one.

Just after one pm Albert rang Mark's telephone number. Albert invited him to the apartment and provided the address. Thirty minutes later Mark climbed out of a local minicab and was greeted by Albert who led him into the sitting area of the flat.

'Coffee, tea or something stronger, Mark?' asked Albert.

'I'll just have some water, please, Albert.'

Both men sat down at a low table in the living area. They sat opposite each other and Albert waited for Mark to open up the conversation.

'First things first, Albert. You know me as Mark but my real name and surname is Marker. My first name is David and I am a Detective Inspector at Forest Gate police station.'

Albert's jaw dropped and he couldn't muster a reply.

'I have had a healthy interest in what has been happening in your old area because my mother lives in Stratford. You used to take her dog for a walk until those bastards strung the dog up from a tree. I try to visit my mum every Sunday if I can. After seeing her I got into the habit, before having lunch with my mum, to have a couple of pints at the Princess Victoria. When I told the publican my name he misheard me so, in there, I have always been known as Mark. It wasn't a problem.'

'Well, to say I am shocked is an understatement. I'm struggling to take all of this in. So, McEvoy is one of your men, then?' asked Albert.

'He is. John and I hold a similar view about everything that has been happening. We both felt for you when you were attacked. As you know, because of the apathy and fear

207

shown by the locals there was nothing we could do. But when they killed my mother's dog we were hoping for a reaction. By getting rid of Trax, you and your merry band have done the local community a favour. None of you will get knighted or receive CBE's although if it was down to John or I, we would have you all at Buckingham Palace in the morning.'

Albert stared at Marker waiting for the next bombshell.

'Everything was going so smoothly. Trax had been disposed of, and we'll come on to that in a minute. Then the gangs started on each other and John McEvoy and I were quite content to let it flow. That is, until we had the Wild West shootout. That was a bit of a worry but we seem to have dodged a bullet with this as well. Did you see what I did there? Dodged a bullet?

'What do you mean?' asked Albert.

'The media have put it all down to gang warfare over drugs and territory. You and your accomplices have ducked nicely under the radar. There doesn't appear to be anything forensically that puts you at the scene of the gunfight and whatever there was, I've managed to take care of it.'

'I don't know what you are talking about.'

'Albert, don't take me for a mug. I will go through a few snippets of evidence and circumstantial bits and pieces which could have you, and your gang locked up for life. I can prove that when Trax went missing you hired a canal boat from a firm in Bethnal Green. I am certain that the narrow boat will still contain evidence of the corpse if it was to be forensically examined. Your next-door neighbour's car was spotted at the canal by a do-gooder who rang in. That's what put me onto the canal boat theory. John McEvoy was able to keep the lid on this information. The cleaning van belonging to Lech was seen making itself busy on various dates at the rear entrance of the pub. If I was to forensicate the cellar at the Princess Victoria I am pretty sure that trace evidence of some description would be uncovered. Shall I continue?'

'Yes, I think you should. Hard evidence is lacking but keep going.'

'On the night that the motorbike rider wrapped himself around a lamp post, a bus driver spotted a dark saloon coming out of that turning. Now, I'm not a betting man but I've got a feeling in my water that the car in question belongs to East London's finest publican and that evidence of contact would still exist on that car. Are you still with me?'

Albert nodded.

'I know that you have been lodging at the pub. I could guarantee you that there would be evidence of gunshot residue found somewhere in that room. You and the others have had the motive to have embarked on clearing up all the shit in the area and let me say straight away that the clear-up was required. In fact, John McEvoy and myself have done quite well out of this. We are very pleased with you. My promotion prospects have taken a turn for the better and John and I are likely to move on to pastures new. We will be a formidable team continuing the fight against crime.'

'I don't accept anything you say, Mister Marker, but if it is true what you are telling me, then why am I not in some

Spanish police cell, awaiting extradition?'

'Albert, John and I are ambitious. There is a loose end or two to tie up in Stratford but we can both see that you could be of some assistance to us when we move on to another patch in London. You have perfected the art of fighting back against criminality and your help would be appreciated. Your reward will be that you retain your freedom. I can't expose you now as that would show my deviousness. The downside is that you will have to spend some time in London away from this blissful hideaway.'

'I completely and utterly deny complicity in any crime,' said Albert, 'and I would like to know what happens now.'

'I will be returning to the UK. I will be in touch with you to let you know when I require your services. The Spanish Guarda Civil are aware of my interest in you and will monitor your movements. I'm going to call a cab. I will be in touch. Good luck, Albert.'

'Before you go.' said Albert, 'How could I not have seen you at your mother's house for all those years?'

'I only saw her on a Sunday. You were probably already in the pub and I always used her side gate and back door.'

Albert saw Marker off the premises. He was dumbfounded. He retrieved the machinery he had bought earlier in the day from the Spanish electrical hardware shop.

It had been taped to the underside of the coffee table. Albert prayed that it had functioned properly and was relieved to see the spools still turning. He sat on the balcony and played back the conversation.

Albert's first port of call was a return to the electrical shop. He was fortunate enough to deal with an assistant who spoke better English than the Spanish that Albert was grappling with. Albert was able to convey that he wanted three copies of the recording and that they should be transferred onto individual USB memory sticks.

Once this had been completed to Albert's satisfaction he pocketed his purchases and wandered down to the Marina where he sat with a glass of San Miguel and reflected on that day's events.

Marker's position was weak. By not arresting Albert or any of his crew he had made himself complicit in crime and although he wasn't up to his neck in the same mire as Albert, his career and possible freedom was under threat. Albert felt pleased that he had in his possession incriminating evidence against Marker. How he would deploy this evidence was still to be decided.

54.

East London Gazette

The funeral of Safiq Mohammed took place yesterday. Safiq Mohammed was one of the youths gunned down in a night of mayhem in East London where four youths lost their lives. Mohammed's uncle, Abdul, told the Gazette, 'He was a very good boy, a very gentle person. He has got mixed up with the wrong crowd. He was studying to be a doctor. It's a tragedy'...

Seven days later the Ryanair jet taxied on the runway at Stansted airport. The flight from Alicante had been smooth until flying through some turbulence just before landing. Albert looked out of the window and saw that the weather was not quite as he had left it in Spain. Dark rain clouds had replaced an unbroken blue sky but at least it was still dry.

Albert passed through Border Control with a minimum amount of clothing contained in a canvas bag and made his way to a connecting bus route which would take him to Stratford.

From the coach drop off he took a taxi to a small hotel on Romford Road in Forest Gate.

He paid for a few nights' stay in advance. The hotel was dingy and the bespectacled weed of a male receptionist was not the best example of sartorial elegance. Nevertheless, it was somewhere to sleep and to attempt to put a plan into action. Albert telephoned Detective Constable John McEvoy on his mobile phone.

'I need to speak to you about something which is of great importance and something which will greatly affect you, personally. It is also important that you don't say anything to David Marker. I want to meet you somewhere private where we can have a civilised discussion. It is important you come on your own. Keep your phone handy and I will ring you at seven pm.'

At first John McEvoy did not recognise the caller ID on his phone but realised quickly that the caller was Albert Oxford.

'Okay,' he replied, 'I'll wait for your call.'

..

At five minutes past seven, Albert rang McEvoy.

'Get yourself on a Docklands Light Railway train and get off at Canning Town. When you get there, wait outside the station. Ring me on this number when you get there.'

'Okay.'

Thirty-five minutes later McEvoy exited Canning Town

station and waited outside on the footway. He rang the number which he presumed to belong to Albert Oxford.

'I'm here,' he said

'Cross over the road and turn right. About four hundred yards away on the left-hand side you will see a Chinese restaurant. I will be waiting there.'

McEvoy walked across the road and spotted the Chinese restaurant in the distance. It stood out, not only because of the garish red lights advertising its presence, but also because every other building in the vicinity was shrouded in darkness and was either closed for business or had shut down.

McEvoy opened the door of the restaurant. The only customer was Albert Oxford who sat at a table away from the small bar. Albert Oxford was facing the restaurant's street door. McEvoy took off his coat and placed it on one of the two vacant chairs next to the table. He sat down opposite Albert.

A diminutive Chinese waiter hovered, but Albert waved him away.

'Not yet, unless you want something to drink, Mister McEvoy?' asked Albert.

'I'll have a beer, thanks, I'm intrigued, Mister Oxford. What do you want to talk to me about?'

'Please call me Albert.' He asked the waiter for two beers.

Albert waited until the beers had been served and the waiter had retired back behind the bar. McEvoy noted that the restaurant was deserted and wondered how such places existed.

Albert Oxford stared at the waiter and he retired to the kitchen.

Albert looked McEvoy in the eye and said, 'I have recently had a conversation with your Detective Inspector, David Marker.'

McEvoy's look of surprise suggested to Albert that the young detective had been unaware of the meeting between Marker and Albert.

'It took place in Spain. Let me tell you straight away that I recorded the conversation. Marker doesn't know, obviously, that I recorded this conversation. I have made three copies of the tape recording. One I have lodged with my Spanish solicitor along with a set of instructions should I come to an untimely end. I have left another copy with a friend of mine and I have the third copy here with me now.'

Albert produced a USB memory stick which he placed on the table.

'I hope you will take my word that our conversation is not being recorded. It doesn't really matter whether you take my word or not, actually, because I am going to tell you the gist of this conversation and then invite you to respond.'

McEvoy sipped nervously at his beer and waited for Albert to speak.

'Marker told me he knew of my complicity in acts of murder. I denied this. He listed a string of facts which could be classified as purely circumstantial evidence which he knew would never secure a conviction of me, or anybody associated with me. He said that you, and he, suppressed evidence in the enquiry into the disappearance of Trax and also withheld evidence into the murders of six people.'

McEvoy groaned audibly and looked distinctly uncomfortable. He took another nervous sip of beer.

'The reason for his actions, he said, was that he was quite happy for these people to have been disposed of as they were partly responsible for the death of his mother's dog. He seems to me to be mentally unhinged and would be a lifetime's work for a decent psychiatrist. His other reason for not doing anything about attempting to solve the murders was to lay the way open for me, and possibly others, to help him rid society of the scum of the earth in whatever part of London he was serving. His trusty lieutenant in all of this is you, Mr McEvoy'

McEvoy remained silent and stared at the floor. He muttered, 'He is unhinged. He's always been fixated about the gang presence in his part of London and he's always happy to see them wiping each other out. He obviously went mental when he heard about the dog. He's dragged me along with him. I didn't want to rock the boat. I have a wife and two young kids. He is due to be promoted and transferred to another part of the Metropolitan Police area. He was going to take me with him when we moved on to another Division. I was hoping that a change of air and scenery would settle him down and we could return to normality. But, of course, this changes things dramatically.'

Albert shouted to the kitchen for two more beers and the waiter shuffled out with a tray and two glasses of beer.

'What happens now?' asked McEvoy

'In a perfect world where Marker finds out I have a hold on him, I would be allowed to return to Spain and continue quietly with the rest of my life. In that same perfect world, you would continue to be industrious on behalf of the Metropolitan Police and you would continue to care for and look after your family. The only problem is that because of the complex Detective Inspector Marker we both know that this isn't going to happen.'

'Detective Chief Inspector. He's been earmarked for promotion and a move is imminent.' replied McEvoy.

Albert Oxford replied, 'I am certain that he won't allow my wish to happen. He will pester the life out of me to do his asking. I can't allow this to happen. I am going to have to put a stop to him. I feel sorry for you. He's manipulated you. As a result of this tape, you could spend the rest of your life behind bars. You need to think of your wife and kids.'

McEvoy was silent for a few seconds. He looked distinctly uncomfortable.

'What would be your plan?' asked McEvoy eventually.

'I have something in mind, John, but at the moment I am going to keep my cards close to my chest. I have your number and you have mine. I will get in touch with you and let you know. It goes without saying, surely, that you don't inform Marker of this meeting and conversation.'

'No problem, Mister Oxford.'

Both men shook hands. McEvoy picked up his coat and left the restaurant.

Albert paid for the beers. He left the restaurant and went back to his lodgings.

55.

The following morning Albert Oxford walked down Romford Road towards Stratford. He turned into West Ham Lane and sat at the back of a cafe and ordered breakfast. His mobile phone rang and he recognised the number of McEvoy.

'I need to speak to you, Mister Oxford. I haven't slept and I'm going mental with worry.'

'Did you mention anything to Marker?' asked Albert.

'No, not a thing. He's carrying on as if nothing has happened. He's all excited about his promotion. He's been told that his next posting is King's Cross. He said he's going to sort out all the dross in the area. He told me we've got a great future in front of us. He says the sky's the limit.'

'He'll come to a sticky end, eventually,' replied Albert, 'the only problem is that you and I are going to be involved in the mess when everything comes crashing down around his ears. I'm in West Ham Lane at the moment. Meet me outside the Turkish hairdressers in an hour.'

Just under an hour later, Albert spotted McEvoy waiting outside Besmullahs, whose shop advertisement in the window boasted that it was the finest hairdressers in east

London.

'Let's go for a walk-through Stratford shopping centre and then we can have a coffee when we get to the food halls at Westfield shopping centre. We can have a chat on the way.'

Albert set off with McEvoy alongside.

'Do you agree that the only way we can solve this is to terminate Marker?'

McEvoy spun round and looked at Albert with a look of complete astonishment on his face but before he could speak Albert said, 'Your career is at an end; your cosy little family life will be destroyed. You, him and I are looking at spending a substantial part of the rest of our lives behind bars.'

'You certainly know how to cheer a person up,' replied McEvoy, 'but what the fuck are we going to do about it?' asked an exasperated McEvoy.

'I have been giving that a bit of thought.' replied Albert. 'But I will need some assistance from you. Don't worry, you won't be getting your hands dirty. I'll take care of it all myself. I know that I can trust you not to grass me up because I have that tape recording where you, my friend, get a serious mention.'

McEvoy visibly winced.

'Whatever you say. What do you want me to do?'

'At some point in the next few days I will be having a meeting with Marker,' said Albert. 'I need to know about his movements after I ring him to set up this meeting. I don't want you involved in any other way.'

'What do you intend to do?' asked McEvoy

'All in good time,' replied Albert.

The two men walked on in silence and parked themselves at a Cuban coffee shop in Westfield shopping centre.

'Be careful, Mister Oxford, he's an evil man. I've been witness to some of the strokes he's pulled.'

'Thank you, John, I will do my best.'

Once coffee had been drunk and McEvoy had settled the bill, both men shook hands and went their separate ways.

56.

Albert rang John McEvoy the next morning just after ten o'clock in the morning.

'Is he in his office?' asked Albert.

'No, he's swanning about at Scotland Yard this morning. He's due back this afternoon,' replied McEvoy.

'Text me when he's back in his office. I want to hear his reaction when I play parts of the tape recording.'

'No problem,' replied McEvoy.

..

Later that day Albert Oxford's phone pinged with a message, '*He's back and he's parked up in his office.*'

Albert had spent the morning after speaking to McEvoy preparing an abridged version of the tape recording with Marker. He used a mobile phone app designed for that purpose.

He dialled the Police station switchboard and asked to be put through to Detective Inspector Marker. He was using a burner phone he had purchased at the shopping market in Stratford. After a lengthy wait, Marker answered

221

his office telephone, 'Marker here.'

Albert held his device with the truncated recording next to the mouthpiece.

'Albert, don't take me for a mug. I will go through a few snippets of evidence and circumstantial bits and pieces which could have you, and your gang, locked up for life... John McEvoy was able to suppress this information... You and the others have had the motive to have embarked on clearing up all the shit in the area and let me say straight away that the clear up was required. In fact, John McEvoy and myself have done quite well out of this. My promotion prospects have taken a turn for the better and John and I are likely to move on to pastures new, as a team, to continue the fight against crime... Albert, John and I are ambitious. There is a loose end or two to tie up in Stratford but we can both see that you could be of some assistance to us when we move on to another patch in London. You have perfected the art of fighting back against criminality and your help would be appreciated. Your reward will be that you retain your freedom. The downside is that you will have to spend some time in London away from this bliss-ful hideaway...

The monitored tape recording had been listened to in complete silence. When it ended Marker very calmly said, 'Oxford, you are a fucking dead man. I will hunt you down and get rid of you.'

'Only problem is, doughnut, that I have three full copies of the tape. One is with a Spanish solicitor, one with a friend and I have the other one, part of which you have just heard. I'm calling the shots now, so just shut the fuck up. You and I need to have a civilised chat and discuss the way

222

forward. There is no way I'm doing you any favours and you can forget all about threatening me. Do I make myself clear?'

'You'll live to regret this,' replied Marker, 'or should I say, you won't live, full stop.'

'We'll see.' replied Albert and he then terminated the phone call.

Albert then texted a message to McEvoy which simply said, '*Ring me this evening at about seven.*'

..

Marker stormed out of his office screaming,

'McEvoy, get in here.'

When John McEvoy entered Marker's office he saw that his Tassimo coffee machine was lying broken on the floor with dark patches of coffee staining the carpet. A coat stand had fallen over, papers and files had obviously been thrown at a wall disturbing an old photograph of uniformed policemen sitting in three neat rows.

'We have a major problem that needs to be sorted. Our friend has gone rogue and is threatening to bring down our little bit of empire building.'

'What do you mean guvnor?' asked McEvoy.

'I paid him a visit in Spain and the shit recorded the conversation. He says he has copies, so he needs to be terminated. He wants to have a meeting with me but he's made a serious mistake. I'll take him out of play.'

Later that day Albert Oxford rang Marker in his office and

arranged to meet him during late afternoon in the bar of a swanky hotel in Covent Garden.

Marker smiled to himself and took out of his office safe, a small handgun and secreted it in the pocket of his overcoat which was hanging from the coat stand which had regained its upright position.Marker knew that the West End, and Soho in particular, would be busy, packed with punters and tourists. He would lay in wait for Oxford outside the hotel and take him down outside the hotel.

He was worried about the tape recordings but had 'friends' in the Spanish Policia who would hunt down the solicitors who had possession of the copy of the tape lodged in Spain. Marker surmised that the tape which had been deposited with a friend would amount to nothing as it compromised that particular person participating in a series of murders. But he suspected that no such friend existed.

John McEvoy sat at his desk pretending to be busy on his computer terminal but at the same time keeping a watchful eye on the office door of his Detective Inspector.

57.

Albert Oxford made his way by London Underground where he alighted at Holborn Underground Station. He remained in the Underground complex and walked towards the platform that would carry passengers south from Holborn station.

Even though packed trains hammered into the station every minute, the platform remained a heaving, pushing mass of people, anxious to get home or desperate to get out of the confines of the rail network in anticipation of an evening's entertainment in the centre of London's social hub.

As a train thundered into the platform from the darkness of the tunnel, headlights blazing, the platform crowd jostled and pushed in an attempt to gain a position near where the doors of the train would open after it had squealed to a halt.

When the doors were opened a mass of commuters would disgorge themselves onto the platform to begin their fight through crowds already pouring down steps onto the platform. Before the next train arrived the platform was already jam packed with people and so the whole process was repeated.

Marker left the police station and walked to the underground station. He had worked out how long it would take him to get to the hotel and knew that he had to change trains at Holborn Tube station. He turned up the collar of his long dark overcoat and pulled down his flat cap firmly onto his head.

He strode purposely onwards with his focus on the task ahead. He did not look round, which was just as well for John McEvoy who had left the police station just after Marker and was now following him from a distance of between fifty and a hundred yards.

Although it was raining lightly there were still plenty of shoppers and pedestrians on the streets. He followed Marker down into the bowl of the tube station, making sure that he wasn't spotted. He kept plenty of commuters between Marker and himself.

When Marker jumped onto the first train heading west, McEvoy boarded the train in an adjoining carriage. The train was packed with passengers but McEvoy was able to push himself through to the door connected to the next carriage. Through the glass window he spotted Marker holding on to an overhead support rail.

When the train was approaching Holborn, it looked as though Marker was preparing to get off the train as he had moved himself towards one of the exit doors.

Marker did indeed alight from the train and proceeded to make his way to the Piccadilly Line platform which would carry him south to Covent Garden. If Marker had turned round he would have spotted McEvoy about twenty yards behind him.

Albert Oxford had positioned himself near the entrance to the platform but had deliberately kept himself away from the platform edge. He used the heaving masses as cover, but focused his eyes on the entrance, hopefully waiting for the appearance of Marker.

And then, suddenly, Marker appeared in shot. Marker fought his way through the massed crowd towards the edge of the platform. Albert, still using the crowd as cover, got himself into a position behind Marker on the platform.

Looking to his left he was staggered to see the figure of Detective Constable John McEvoy. McEvoy did not spot Albert Oxford but appeared to be focusing his attention on Marker.

McEvoy looked up at the flashing neon signs which displayed 'TRAIN APPROACHING' and heard the thunderous rumbling roar of the oncoming train which was preceded by a rush of warm foetid air.McEvoy moved forward and started pushing the large woman in front of him. She was powerless to resist the surge and therefore forced forward pressure onto Marker.

Marker attempted to resist but was struggling to maintain his balance. The noise of the train grew louder as it screamed into the platform space. Marker looked round in panic and saw McEvoy pushing a fat lady towards him.

He swiftly removed the handgun from his overcoat and pointed the pistol at McEvoy and fired.

Even above the noise of the approaching train, people screamed and pushed each other in a mad scramble to get away from the gunman. The fat lady slipped, losing her balance and knocked Marker onto the rail tracks.

Albert Oxford watched everything as if everything was being acted out in slow motion. As Marker fell backwards onto the track Albert was sure that Marker was looking at him.

Marker flailed his arms and legs as he hit the track. The approaching train thundered into the station accompanied by a squeal of brakes and people screaming.

The train wheels sliced the body of David Marker into three separate pieces and pulled up just before the platform exit. The concourse suddenly emptied of people.

Albert Oxford and a few stragglers saw the apparently lifeless body of John McEvoy lying on the platform with a neat, red-rimmed hole in the middle of his forehead.

Albert Oxford calmly stepped aboard the upward escalator. At the top he passed through the barrier and stepped out in the fresh air of the Kingsway and walked south towards the Aldwych.

Before jumping onto a 25 bus which would take him back to Romford Road he grabbed a takeaway cup of coffee. He took a seat in the rarefied atmosphere up on the top deck of the bus and attempted to get his head round what had happened.

McEvoy had stolen his show and had done what he himself was going to do. Albert Oxford now realised that Marker had been armed. McEvoy's actions had saved him. Albert had dodged a bullet, literally.

But why had McEvoy carried out an attempted execution? McEvoy had hinted that Marker was unhinged and therefore posed a threat to McEvoy's future. That could be the only explanation. Everything had fallen neatly into Albert's lap.

The journey back to Stratford took forever because of the rush hour traffic but Albert sat contentedly taking in the scenery as he passed through the parts of London he knew very well. It was almost a lap of honour and a last goodbye to the city he had been born in, grew up in, and worked in. The city had provided him with a living which allowed him to house himself and cherish the woman he had been married to.

58.

ack in his digs in East London, Albert sat with one eye on the television news channel and one ear tuned into a small transistor radio waiting for the fallout from the incident at Holborn underground station. However, both news outlets appeared to be concentrating on the spread of a killer virus which had originated in China and was now in the process of spreading worldwide. Apart from China the virus was now rapidly spreading round Europe with epicentres in Italy, Spain and France.

The news reports were saying that it was only a matter of time before the disease hopped across the channel and attacked the United Kingdom. Death rates abroad were high and the British Government, who at first had been too complacent, were now expressing concern about the spread.

At the end of the respective bulletins there was mention of an incident at a London Underground station which had closed the station and was being investigated by British Transport Police.

59.

Metro Newspaper

British Transport Police are investigating the
deaths of two men at Holborn Underground
Station on Tuesday evening. The two men are
both thought to be serving members of the Criminal Investigation Department with the Metropolitan Police. A Scotland Yard spokesman told this
newspaper that it would not be commenting on
the case until enquiries had been completed...

Albert Oxford spent most of the next three days holed up
in his room. He listened intently to every scrap of news
and when he did leave his room, it was to grab some breakfast at a local cafe and to scoop up the daily newspapers
which he scoured from front to back.

The tube station story was relegated to the inside pages
as news of the spreading pandemic took up most of the
space on the first four or five pages.

One newspaper report on the two deaths intimated that

the two men were known to each other. It was thought that a firearm had been involved. The two dead men had not been named and Scotland Yard and the British Transport police were not commenting on the incident.

Albert decided to pay a visit to his three compatriots in crime. His first port of call was to his ex-neighbour Harry who ushered him into the kitchen where he put the kettle on.

'How are your new neighbours, Harry?' asked Albert.

'They're from Afghanistan, Albert. Six kids, noisy. We were planning to move down to live near the wife's sister so this has just made the move a little bit more pressing.'

'I'm sorry Harry. I had a look at the place on my way in. At least it looks better than the last time I saw it with all that smoke damage.'

'Since I last saw you Albert, you have been a little busy. Lech told me all about the gunfight at the OK Corral.'

'Harry, did you know that Mark from the pub on a Sunday morning was Old Bill? His mum is old Mo Connors who lives across the road from you. He and another copper were crooked. They were manipulating me, indirectly, to clear up all the shit in this area. But they had a coming together at Holborn tube station and they are both brown bread. That means I have a good chance of getting away with this. I'm going to fuck off back to Spain. I hope everything works out for you Harry'

'That was obviously the two mysterious deaths at the tube station, then?'

Albert nodded.

'Look after yourself, mate. Don't let the virus get you.

Stay safe.'

They looked into each other's eyes and firmly shook hands. On leaving, Albert took a last long lingering look at the place where he had spent his married life. Happy memories up until the last few months. He felt desperately sad that it had come to this and thought that if he had his time again he would still have got involved in the fight-back.

Albert's next port of call was to his big Polish friend. Lech invited him in and they sat down in comfortable armchairs in the small living room.

'I'm off, Lech.' said Albert. 'I've had enough of this area, this city and this country. I don't know how we've got away with it, but it looks like we have. I'm disappearing to Spain. Mark from the pub was a bent copper who was manipulating me and the others. His mate was that Detective McEvoy, but they have contrived to kill each other. I witnessed it all but wasn't involved. It was Mark's plan to kill me because I had incriminating evidence against him.'

Lech stared at Albert, mouth open and slack jawed.

'When are you leaving, Albert?' asked Lech.

'Because of this virus thing the flights to Spain are a bit hit and miss and I need to make sure that everything is neat and tidy at this end but hopefully in a few days I will be off. What about you, Lech?' asked Albert.

'Annelka and I are going back to Poland. We will adopt at least one child. We were happy in this country but it has gone down the pan, is that how you say it?'

Albert smiled at Lech's command of the English language. Lech continued, 'Nobody in this city wants to protect the ordinary man. The police, the Mayor, they have all abandoned us. We have had to fight back ourselves but it is a losing battle. There will always be somebody to replace Trax and all the other arseholes. If there is nobody to help us, my best move is to head back to my home country with my wife and start to live the rest of my life in peace.'

'I can't argue with that, Lech. You've been a good and loyal friend. I don't blame you for leaving. I'm leaving myself. I'm heading back to Spain. Harry is moving out as well. They've won. Our fightback has all been in vain. They have got rid of us and all because we didn't have the support of the police or the authorities. We've been let down badly. Fuck knows what this part of London will finish up as. Only Eddie will be left. It'll be like Custer's last stand or Rorke's Drift. Poor old Eddie.'

The two men looked at each other and smiled. Lech didn't correlate with Albert's historical references but got the gist of what he was saying.

'We can be proud that we tried to do something, Albert.'

They shook hands and Albert walked off in the direction of the Princess Victoria public house.

Albert walked into the saloon bar and saw that Eddie was busying himself polishing the pint glasses.

'I suppose you've come to tell me that you're doing a runner, Albert?'

'I'm afraid so Eddie. I have no future around here. The Iberian Peninsula beckons. I won't have much of a future there either but it will be warmer and I don't have to deal with all the shit round here.'

'I can't blame you Albert. I'll miss you and your friendship. By the looks of it you'll be leaving soon enough. This virus thing looks like a bit of a worry. They're talking about closing down pubs and restaurants, so that'll be me fucked if that happens. Keep in touch Albert and let me know how you are getting on.'

'I will, Eddie.' replied Albert, 'Take care and look after yourself.' Another emotional handshake followed. Albert had a last look round the pub, briefly remembering all the fun times in the saloon bar but shuddering slightly at the memories of the macabre scenes that took place below ground in the cellar of the pub.

Before leaving Albert looked back into the bar. Eddie was standing with his back to the fireplace with a wistful, sad smile on his face.

Albert decided to walk back to his accommodation in Romford Road. He took in all the sights that brought back memories of the last forty years or so. He couldn't help noticing the scarcity of people on the streets but those that were present were wearing face coverings. Strange times!

Back in his motel room, Albert devoured all the news channels. No more mention of any incident at Holborn Underground Station. All channels were consumed by the invasion of the virus and the gloomy news that the Government was considering locking down the country in an effort to contain the disease.

It was also apparent that the virus was not just contained to the United Kingdom. It had already ripped through

Italy and Spain and the rest of continental Europe was suffering at the hands of this disease imported from China.

Albert checked that flights to and from the continent were still in operation but news reporters were voicing concerns that this situation wouldn't last for much longer. Albert decided there and then that he would fly back to his place in Spain the following day.

60.

As the plane taxied on the runway at Alicante airport, Albert considered the difference between the shimmering haze and the bright blue sea on his left, and what he had left behind on a cold, rainy day in East London.

After picking up his luggage Albert couldn't help but notice that nearly everybody in the airport was wearing a face mask. He clambered into a taxi and noticed that the driver was also wearing a face mask. Albert's command of the Spanish language was not of a sufficiently high standard that would allow him to interrogate the driver about the situation of the growing pandemic in Spain, but Albert already sensed that the virus was at a more advanced stage than it was in the United Kingdom.

The journey back to Albert's apartment did not take long and Albert felt a sense of relief when he saw that the apartment was as he had left it. Everything was still in working order and after sweeping the balcony, removing leaves and a layer of dusty sand, Albert settled down to take in the news from the United Kingdom. He flicked to a Spanish news channel and saw that the programmes were dominated by a growing concern about the spread of the virus.

Albert made himself a cup of tea and went downstairs to check over the Berlingo that provided him with his transport and means of earning money. After a couple of splutters the engine sprung into life emitting a belch of smoke, but after a couple of minutes the engine was ticking over satisfactorily.

Albert decided it was time to stock up on provisions and drove the van to the local supermarket. He was staggered to see a long queue outside the store. The shoppers obviously had the same intention as Albert. It took him far longer than he expected to buy his provisions but he felt happier once he was back at the apartment and his purchases unloaded.

Albert Oxford spent the next few days devouring the television news channels. It was apparent that Spain and other countries were at a more advanced stage than others, including the UK, and it was also clear that sanctions and other measures designed to limit the spread of the virus were likely to be imposed imminently.

Albert rang the company that he did part-time work for. He informed them that he was back in the country and was available for work. The English-speaking manager of the company was able to tell Albert that instead of re-laying customers to and from the airport, the company would be concentrating on the delivery of goods, including food, from a large retail company near the airport.

Albert was keen to get back to work, not only to get out of the apartment, but to subsidise his bank funds. Albert was very happy to take on the early shift as he had never had a problem getting up in the morning but it also left the rest of the day free to do as he wished.

The next few weeks took up a familiar pattern. Albert would drive to the store where he would load up his cargo. A list of drop offs was supplied and, with use of a satellite navigation app on his phone, Albert was able to make his deliveries. He was usually back home just after midday and after showering he would always take the short walk into the seaside town to partake of a light lunch. This was followed by a walk along the front.

It had become apparent to Albert that the flow of pedestrians on the seafront had been greatly reduced because of fears about the pandemic. Those who did stroll were in the main wearing face coverings. After his constitutional walk Albert would make his way back to the apartment and take his fill of all the news from around the world.

The goings-on at Holborn Tube Station had been relegated to obscurity. The business with Trax, Saf and the others seemed like a lifetime ago and Albert was content that their combined fightback against the bullies had seemed to have paid off.

Apart from the inconvenience of this virus, life was proceeding satisfactorily for Albert Oxford. The only cloud on the horizon was news that the Spanish government was intending to impose a lockdown of citizens in an attempt to help suppress the pandemic.

61.

Some weeks later In London, a population under lock down, was beginning to emerge slowly from an enforced hibernation.

William Cronk sat in the early summer sunshine and reflected on his news. His hospital appointment had not gone well but now he was back home sitting in his garden in the sunshine with a glass of chilled white wine. He had the opportunity to cast his mind back on his career in the Police which had come to a natural end a few months back.

He prided himself on having solved everything that had been presented to him, save for the murder of the young black girl at the MacDonald's in Tottenham. He was satisfied that the killer was probably dead but the whole business of the deaths in east London had left an unhappy feeling in the pit of his stomach.

The two detectives, Marker and McEvoy, who had been looking at the east London connection, had both perished under mysterious circumstances which were still reverberating internally around the Metropolitan Police Service. He decided it was time to call in a favour, one of many he was owed by people to whom he had done a favour over the last 30 years.

Three days later a courier rang Cronk's doorbell. When Cronk answered he had to sign for a fairly large cardboard box. As a widower for the last eight years, Cronk had the house to himself so the box was taken to the dining room at the back of the building and he was able to utilise the largely defunct dining table where he carefully emptied the contents of the box.

The documents were dominated by photocopies of filed reports printed from the hard drive of a computer. A separate box file included photographs and copied photographs taken from surveillance cameras and also screenshots from fixed point surveillance cameras as well as copies of stills taken from CCTV cameras.

Cronk decided on a method of poring over these files and chose that the best course was to attack them chronologically. He realised that this would take some considerable time but with no outside pressure save sleep, food, medicines and hospital appointments he could devote all his time to working through the contents of the cardboard box.

He made two phone calls. The first was to an ex-colleague and friend who worked at Criminal Intelligence at New Scotland Yard. The second call was to an old rugby playing compatriot, Dennis, who worked as a private investigator, based in the outskirts of Alicante, Spain. Dennis had spent some time serving in the Metropolitan Police until an unsavoury incident prematurely ended his police career.

William Cronk had taken advantage of Dennis's generous hospitality in the past and had enjoyed the sunshine and Spanish food and beers. The call to Dennis was difficult for Cronk and took some time. Cronk told him of his illness and the prognosis.

62.

lbert Oxford's routine in Spain did not vary much. A typical day saw him driving to his work base, loading up his van with deliveries and spending the morning dropping off those deliveries and goods to people closeted behind doors in an effort to combat the spread of the virus.

When finished, Albert would return to his apartment where he would make himself some lunch whilst catching up on the worldwide news with regards to the pandemic. Lockdowns were gradually being eased around Europe and Albert was able to take advantage of this easing as it allowed him to walk to the seafront and stroll along the paved promenade as far as the small marina.

When there, he would park himself at a table and allow himself a beer whilst taking in the vista in front of him. Single fishermen were dotted along the small jetty. Fishing lines were cast from into a sea of aquamarine. A pleasantly warm breeze wafted along the seafront.

A chilled glass of San Miguel made Albert feel comforted by the decision he had taken to move to Spain. The events of the past few months seemed a world away and he certainly didn't miss the drudgery of the east end of London, nor the weather, nor the criminal element which had forced him and some of his friends to fight back. He wondered how his old friends were faring.

After a couple of beers Albert would walk back to his apartment and prepare his evening meal. Invariably he would then devour the news channels followed by the Sky Sports channels. On two evenings a week Albert attended Spanish language evening classes. This allowed him to mix and socialise but, more importantly, allowed him to communicate in a very basic fashion with his neighbours back at his apartment. Things had worked out okay, Albert mused.

63.

efore leaving home, William Cronk had a lingering last look round his house to ensure that everything had been switched off properly and the house was secure. He placed a sealed envelope in the middle of the dining room table. He closed all the curtains and picked up his small suitcase containing his changes of clothing, his medication and some of the paperwork he had illicitly received from the Criminal Intelligence Department at New Scotland Yard.

He waited by his street door and within seconds his ordered minicab arrived to convey him to Stansted Airport. Some four hours later Cronk's plane was taxiing along the runway at Alicante airport.

After clearing Customs Cronk followed the exit points where he was greeted by a mass of people holding up signs with the names of arriving passengers.

He quickly scanned the sea of bronzed faces. William Cronk immediately recognised the swarthy features of Dennis McMillan, Private Investigator and ex Metropolitan Police officer.

Although it had been some years since he had last seen

Dennis, his battered facial features from an unsuccessful rugby career gave him away.

A big hug and warm handshake followed before McMillan ushered Cronk out to the fourth-floor multi-storey car park and within minutes they had left the airport complex and were heading to the hotel which McMillan had booked for Cronk.

Nothing of any significance was said on the way, save for an explanation of Cronk's physical appearance and an update on William's medical condition. McMillan frowned and placed his free hand on Cronk's knee.

At the hotel, after checking in, both men retired to the room that had been booked for Cronk. McMillan placed on the bed a package wrapped in brown paper and held together by elastic bands.

'What you asked for,' said McMillan. 'Be careful.'

Cronk arranged to meet Dennis McMillan later in the day in the foyer of the hotel.

'I owe you a meal Dennis, and a lot more, but you'll have to settle for a meal for now.'

William Cronk then slept fitfully for a couple of hours. He awoke, showered, and changed into clothes more suitable for the Spanish climate.

64.

Albert Oxford's alarm shattered his deep sleep and after showering he was soon on his way to the depot in his Berlingo.

He was assisted by staff to load his vehicle and after he had been handed a delivery note, he set off to make his drop-offs. The morning's work went smoothly. He found the addresses without difficulty and his progress was only halted temporarily by a stop at a favourite cafe for a fix of coffee and a bocadillo.

He contemplated an afternoon of relaxation in the warm Spanish afternoon sun. Albert finished his deliveries just after noon and drove back to his apartment.

Albert parked his vehicle in his parking space and after entering his apartment he changed into a t-shirt and shorts. He strolled down to the seafront nodding occasionally to various neighbours that he recognised en-route.

Fifteen minutes later he was parked at a table furthest from the cafe but which had a view of the fisherman with lines cast out into the shimmering blue sea. He would have a walk later to inquire how successful their efforts had been.

He ordered a prawn dish and a cold Spanish beer. He removed a Spanish newspaper from his back pocket and attempted to read the paper in an effort to improve his grip on the language. He felt he had made giant strides and was comfortable reading the written word but struggled more when speaking and listening to Spanish as it was usually rattled off at a pace he couldn't keep up with. But, progress was progress, and he was confident he would master it eventually.

After he had finished his lunch and his beer, Albert paid the waitress and got up to walk across to the fishermen to inquire as to their good fortune, or not, with their exploits.

As he stood up he was aware of a tall, gaunt man standing next to him wearing a white linen jacket and chino trousers. He wore a pair of light brown deck shoes.

'Albert Oxford?' asked the stranger.

'Who's asking?' replied Albert

'My name is William Cronk. I want to talk to you about events that have happened in London over the past few months. Let's sit down and have a chat.'

Cronk sat down awkwardly and Albert, with some reluctance, sat opposite him. Albert noticed that Cronk, despite the Spanish heat, had a pale sweaty pallor with eyes that seemed lifeless and sunk deep into his bony face.

Cronk caught the eye of the waitress and ordered a coffee. He didn't offer a drink to the man opposite him. He paid the waitress and took a sip of the coffee. He turned to Albert and said, 'Now let's get down to business. I don't want you to say anything until I have finished. Do you understand?'

'I don't know who you are, or what you are talking about, but carry on. I'll sit here and listen until it's time for me to go home and have my afternoon nap. Crack on.'

'Please let me indulge myself whilst I set out the case. Members of the jury,' started Cronk, 'let me introduce myself. I am prosecuting counsel for this trial at the Central Criminal Court. In the dock before you is one Albert Oxford. He is charged with three counts of murder. There are numerous other charges on the indictment but we will contain ourself for the moment with the counts of murder. I will outline to you now the broad details.'

'Have you just escaped from some mental institution?' asked Albert.

Cronk paused and took another sip of the coffee.

'Albert Oxford, who is before you in the dock, is a middle-aged widower having lost his wife to cancer two years previous to this case. He was living a lonely, but contented life, in his house in east London. He worked part time as a London taxi driver, supported his local football team, and went for a drink, two or three times a week with neighbours and friends. Life for him was untroubled.

'That is, until the balance was upset by a gang of hoodlums operating on his doorstep. Albert Oxford crossed paths with this gang and from that moment his life took on a different, more violent course. With the help of his drinking companions, he set about disposing of the leader of this gang.

'Another gang member followed shortly. He was killed after being discovered following Oxford on his motorcycle. The killings culminated in a firearm shootout known

249

locally as the Gunfight at the OK Corral.'

Cronk paused again for another sip of coffee.

'How am I doing so far?' asked Cronk.

'I've never heard such a load of shit. Who the fuck are you? You're obviously a frustrated actor.'

'My name is Cronk. I'm a retired Detective Superintendent in the Metropolitan Police. I prided myself on the fact that I got to the bottom of every case and solved everything that was put into my care. Although I know everything in your case, it has got up my nose that you are free, sunning yourself in Spain, having escaped justice for the crimes you have committed.'

'Listen, Mr Crock of shit,' replied Albert, 'what mystifies me is this. If you have the evidence you say, why am I not on the plane back to London in handcuffs. Where's your back-up police squad? And where is this mysterious evidence that you have?'

'I don't need back-up. You're not going anywhere. Just sit there and listen. The man Trax, who first messed you up, is undoubtedly at the bottom of the River Lea or the Lea Navigation canal. There is photographic evidence of you attending a canal boat hire company in east London.

'There exists documentary evidence that you hired such a canal boat. A statement was taken from a neighbour describing the movements of you and three others acting suspiciously in the rear yard of the Princess Victoria Public House.

'You were also involved with the death of a gang member who met an unfortunate end when his motorcycle had a coming-together with a lamp post. Witness statements describe the car as one very similar to that of your friend, the publican from the Princess Victoria.

'There are also witness statements describing someone of your build and appearance wearing an outsize Army greatcoat involved in the mass shooting. Another witness describes that person making good his escape by being picked up in a van belonging to your Polish friend. The same van, by the way, that Trax was abducted in.

'I believe that Trax was disposed of near the pub and I'm sure that a full forensic examination of those premises and the van would have convicted all four of you.'

'Then why am I still sitting here?' Albert countered. 'If you've got all this evidence against me, why wasn't it used at the time?'

'Well, that is the problem, Mr Oxford. I was the officer in charge of the Tottenham end of this enquiry but unfortunately the Stratford end was conducted by a man who not only disgraced himself, but disgraced the reputation of the Metropolitan Police, an organisation I have been proud to represent for nearly forty years.

'Not only did he let himself down, but he dragged down a fine young man whose mind he turned. Marker suppressed the evidence to suit his own ends. He controlled that part of London and that investigation was just the tip of his criminal enterprises. McEvoy was a scared young man who was terrified of upsetting Marker. McEvoy thought that he saw an opportunity to get back at him and took it. That is why it ended as it did at Holborn Underground station.

'You do know, don't you, that you were the intended

target? You were captured on closed circuit television, but perhaps you had plans of your own? Unfortunately, because of the actions of Marker, every job and prosecution that he was involved with is now tainted. This means that criminals are being released from prison and every investigation he has touched is being forgotten about. It's a complete embarrassment for the Metropolitan Police and it's all fallen nicely for you. Sadly, it has tarnished the whole of my career and you won't be able to comprehend how sad that has made me.'

Albert Oxford remained silent. He noticed that Cronk was sweating freely.

'What about the others you have mentioned? Have they been nicked?'

'No. As I said, the whole episode has been an embarrassment, not only to me, but to the Metropolitan Police. Your friend, the publican, has succumbed to the virus. He died about three weeks ago on a ventilator in hospital.'

Albert was shocked. Eddie had been a real friend. The man who said he had taken on the Taliban and the IRA singlehanded had been beaten by Coronavirus.

'What about the others?' asked Albert.

'Your Polish friend has returned to Poland with his wife. The Polish authorities have been alerted to the probability that he has been involved in serious criminal activities. His existence and lifestyle will be closely monitored.'

Albert was shaken. He had been pleased for Lech and Annelka in their mission to foster children back in their home country, but obviously that wouldn't happen now that the authorities in Poland would be combing through their life in east London.

'And as for your neighbour, Harry, he has moved out of the area to live in Essex. Reports tell me that he is not a well man and is suffering from an ailment that may foreshorten his existence. So, that just leaves you, Mr Oxford. I have a modicum of sympathy for you. You were threatened by a criminal element which was affecting the life of you, your neighbours and your friends. You could not rely on the services of the local police because of their own criminality, so you decided to take the law into your own hands. That decision has resulted directly, and indirectly, in the loss of several lives.'

Albert noticed that during this delivery Cronk struggled to speak coherently and his narrative was paused on occasions for Cronk to take in gulps of air. Regaining his composure, he continued, 'I've tracked you down with the assistance of an old friend of mine. It's inconceivable to me that you should be able to get away with what you have done. Although I am officially retired I would be failing in my duty as a man if you were allowed to remain free.'

Once again Cronk paused for breath. Albert Oxford wondered what the next move would be. He guessed that the person sitting opposite him was not very well. His complexion had gone a deathly pale and he appeared to be gasping for breath.

Albert looked around him. The other tables surrounding them were unoccupied. The fishermen on the jetty in the distance were still holding onto fishing lines, hoping to land that evening's repast. Seagulls hovered, then swooped, squawking at the fishermen, their shrieks disturbing the stillness of the afternoon.

The long spiky fronds of the regimental palm trees along the wide promenade rustled and whispered in the breeze. The seagulls settled on the railing by the side of the jetty.

'What happens now?' asked Albert.

'I'm not very well,' replied Cronk, 'but thanks to some friends who have returned favours, I have accumulated a welter of evidence against you. I have spent the last few weeks of my life sifting through files and photographs sent to me at my home. Admittedly a lot of the evidence is circumstantial and witnesses will not be able to be relied on. Unfortunately, I only have a limited amount of time left, not enough to see you possibly convicted, so I have taken the decision to take matters into my own hands. Ironically, similar to what you did yourself back in London.'

Cronk paused for breath again.

'The Crown Prosecution Service will not authorise your arrest and prosecution because of the involvement of Marker. I cannot allow you to get away with this.'

Cronk stood up, shakily, and from the inside pocket of his jacket he produced a handgun.

Albert Oxford froze and found himself staring at Cronk's finger on the trigger. Everything seemed to happen in slow motion. Oxford saw the flash, followed by a searing pain on his left temple. He fell to the ground and lay motionless.

He could still see. He thought he must still be alive. The fishermen had stopped casting into the sea and were all looking in his direction. He heard a female, presumably the waitress, screaming.

As his head rested on the sandstone paving he could see his blood trickling away from him and settling into the cracks in the paving.

Whilst he was lying there, desperately trying to assess the situation, he heard another gunshot and in that instant a human head landed with a thump onto the paving stone next to him.

Cronk's face was twisted in pain but apart from that, it looked normal. Normal, that is, apart from the gaping cavity at the back of his skull where a mass of fluid and fragments of bone had spilled onto the ground beside him.

Albert couldn't move. His head lay next to that of Cronk. Before the blackness descended on Albert Oxford he could hear, in the distance, the sound of sirens.

65.

SIX MONTHS LATER

Albert Oxford opened the door to his accommodation and after putting on the kettle he sat down in his comfortable armchair. He reflected on the past six months.

After the trauma of his shooting and Cronk's suicide, he had been taken unconscious to the Spanish hospital where he remained for two weeks.

The bullet fired by Cronk had only struck him with a glancing blow. Cronk was in the final throes of his life due to the invasive cancer that had attacked his body. He had looked shaky when speaking to Albert and this had obviously affected his steadiness and his aim. Cronk had been sure he had mortally wounded Oxford and had then taken his own life.

During his stay in hospital Albert had been visited by various authorities. Two detectives from the Spanish Guardia Civil sat by his bedside in the room in the hospital which had been set aside for his stay. The interpreter was superfluous to requirements as Albert refused to answer any questions.

Albert was visited on more than one occasion and on the last of these visits he was informed by the interpreter that the Spanish police had no reason to detain him but that the Spanish authorities did not want him to remain in Spain and that he was to be repatriated to the UK as soon as the hospital doctors were satisfied that he was fit to leave hospital and travel.

Albert Oxford was given a week to tidy up his affairs in Spain. His property was placed in the hands of a Spanish estate agent to sell on his behalf. He was required to inform the local Policia of the date, time and flight number from Alicante airport to Stansted.

On arrival at Stansted, he was met by two officers from the Metropolitan Police and taken to a north London police station. There he had been interviewed for an hour.

Albert had been very non-committal and the senior of the two officers informed him that he was free to go but on condition that he furnished the police with his current address. This would be a problem as Albert explained he had no fixed abode but he eventually supplied them with the old lodgings from Forest Gate and promised them he would update them when he had secured somewhere permanent.

And so it was that Albert sat back in his chair with a mug of tea. He wondered to himself if he had gotten away with it. It certainly appeared to be so. The Spaniards were not interested in him and had treated him as a victim of crime. Albert had felt put out that they didn't want him living in their country. Maybe it was something to do with the trail of bodies he had been responsible for in the United Kingdom.

As for the Metropolitan Police, he pondered why he was still free, especially after hearing from Cronk the alleged evidence against him. He could only surmise that the reason for this was the fact that the whole investigation and resulting evidence, had been tainted by the involvement of Marker and to a lesser extent, McEvoy. Scotland Yard and the Home Office would be embarrassed by the stain made by those two individuals. It was conceivable that all the cases that these two had been involved in were being re-examined causing maximum discomfort to the authorities.

On many occasions since his return from Spain Albert had reflected on what had happened during the last eighteen months, or so. Was it all worth it? Would he do it again given the opportunity? He didn't know the answer to that. He had lost some friends but they would probably have gone in any event. They had been loyal, true friends and they had all been united in their desire to fight back against brutal bullying and unrestrained violence.

Albert sat back in his chair and felt his leg being nudged. He looked down and stroked the furry head of his newly adopted friend. Pleading eyes sitting above a glistening wet nose always melted Albert's resolve. He picked up the dog's lead. Bart's tail wagged furiously.

Albert secured the door to his premises and walked along the gangway and followed the dog by stepping from the canal boat onto the towpath. He let the dog off his leash and Bart raced on taking in the smells of his evening walk.

Albert was back in his part of London. On his dog walking routine, he was able to walk past the shell of the stadium where his football team played. No crowd noises due to pandemic restrictions but that wouldn't be forever.

When he walked from his boat through the canal-side buildings to the little supermarket, the vast majority of people he met were wearing face masks. But that wouldn't be forever.

The supermarket provided him with his home comforts. He contented himself with reading, listening to classical music and partaking of a glass or two of his favourite red wine. He had become a half decent cook but on occasions would treat himself to a meal in an Italian restaurant just a few streets away. He would sometimes have lunch at the riverside pub which had brought back memories of his friends.

On a couple of occasions, he had visited a public house in Hackney called the Plume of Feathers. The clientele included a few interesting characters and the bonhomie in the pub had reminded him of happier times spent in the Princess Victoria with Lech and Eddie. The regulars in the Plume of Feathers had readily accepted Albert into their midst.

He had found this decent public house on the Hackney side of the canal where now, with restrictions being slowly eased, he could have a decent Sunday lunchtime pint whilst discussing events on the football pitches up and down the country. The sale of his property in Spain had realised him enough profit to sustain a decent lifestyle aboard his canal boat. He had been very lucky. Life at the moment was good.

Bart came running back to him. The dog looked disturbed. Further along the towpath he saw a group of youths huddled in conversation. As he passed them one of the group called out, 'Hey, old man, hope you're picking up your dog's shit.'

Albert hesitated, turned up the collar of his coat and walked on.

66.

Two days earlier, Dennis McMillan had flown back to the United Kingdom. Some months had passed since his old friend, William Cronk, had perished in the Spanish seafront town.

McMillan had recovered the firearm from the scene before the Spanish Police had arrived to investigate. McMillan had known of Cronk's intention to kill Oxford but after the shooting had been unprepared for Cronk's taking of his own life. McMillan was also stunned and enraged by the fact that Oxford had appeared to have survived the attempt on his life.

McMillan had swiftly scooped up the firearm and document file and made good his escape through the small church situated between the restaurants and shops. He went through the church and exited by the rear door and then made his way to his car parked at the rear.

His next stop was to Cronk's hotel and a tidy up of his room. He paid Cronk's bill at reception.

Now, Dennis McMillan was in the UK to complete his old friend Cronk's unfinished business. Squatting in the bushes, tucked completely out of sight from prying eyes, he kept observation on a canal boat moored on the Lea Navigation Canal.

Over the course of the next few days, McMillan was able to chart Albert Oxford's habits. Oxford's lifestyle was simple. He walked his Jack Russell dog along the towpath on a regular basis.

Albert Oxford sometimes left the boat on his own but always returned with shopping bags. On one occasion Oxford cast off and took his craft up the canal. The dog sat proudly at the prow of the boat barking at anyone who dared to walk or cycle along the towpath. McMillan worried that Albert Oxford had decided on a change of scenery but his anxiety was be-calmed when he spotted the craft, with Captain Birdseye on the bow still barking at passers-by. The canal boat was secured and life continued as before for those aboard the canal boat.

Later that day, as the late afternoon sun dropped down below the height of the trees, and the dusk slowly turned into darkness, McMillan saw that Albert had emerged from the boat with the dog and, as was his habit at this time of the day, took the dog for a short walk before retiring for the night.

McMillan was aware of this habit and this gave him enough time to remove from his rucksack the rifle parts. He quickly assembled them. He fitted a silencer and telescopic sight.

McMillan saw Albert Oxford and Bart returning to the boat. The dog skipped onto the deck and as Albert Oxford stepped onto the deck a sharp crack could be heard. The left temple of Albert Oxford seemed to have exploded.

McMillan saw that he had shot Oxford through the ear and presumed that Oxford was already dead before he hit the deck and fell overboard into the water. The dog barked, continuously, at his master to get up, but to no avail.